MW01593548

EST. 2021

www.bagofbonespress.com

A HORROR ANTHOLOGY - 206 WORD STORIES
Copyright 2022 Bag of Bones Press
All Rights Reserved

Thank you to everyone involved in the making of this book.
Copyright of each piece belongs to the individual author.

Cover art by TT Tucker, SJ Townend & Bag of Bones
Press.

Internal art: Jak MCS Tattoos & Artwork
www.gnarlydungeon.com

Stories compiled and edited by SJ Townend
First edition: March 2022

ISBN: 978-1-7397419-0-7

Disclaimer & Copyright

Bag of Bones Press

A Horror Anthology
206 Word Stories

by various contributors

A collection of bone-chilling tales by authors from all over the world.

Content Warnings:

<u>This book is recommended for adults only.</u>

Themes of murder, violence, assault, death, infant death, gore, blasphemy, and abuse are dotted throughout. Please be aware, this book may shock.

British and American spellings are found within this book.

About the Editor:

SJ Townend lives in Bristol, UK with her family. She has had several pieces of horror and speculative fiction published through a variety of presses. When not reading, writing, or editing, you might find her teaching science to trainee medics, parenting her two smalls, or following the cat around the house.

Find her on Twitter: @SJTownend

We challenged our contributors to write a piece of horror with 206 words—one for each bone of the adult body. Our inbox was flooded with hundreds of amazing stories. We chose 206 of them to publish here, for your enjoyment; a story for each bone.

If you enjoy writing, please check out our website for our current submission calls:
www.bagofbonespress.com/submission-calls

This book is dedicated to everyone who submitted a story for this, our first, Bag of Bones project.

TABLE OF CONTENTS

Forgotten by Steve Bridger – 12

The Stairway of Tartarus by Miguel Ángel López – 14

Whatever Happened to Sycorax? by Syreeta Muir – 16

Lithopedion by Christina Ladd – 18

The Red Line by Jacob Osterhaus – 20

Parasite by Tejaswinee Roychowdhury – 22

Glean by Lindz McLeod – 24

The Voice by Axl Malton – 26

Exactly Like Them by Guan Un – 28

An Evolution of Design by Patricia Miller – 30

It's All In Hand by Charlie Brigden – 32

Inseparable by R D Doan – 34

Being an Elf by Alison Long – 36

Homegrown by Eric Netterlund – 38

Actually, Miss Jane, I Like It... by M. Roanoke – 40

The Shadow by Betsy Nicchetta – 42

Ding-Dong Ditch by Riley Odell – 44

Cold Caller by Malcolm Timperley – 46

The Creature by Aaron Murphy – 48

Give a Dog a Bone by Benjamin Langley – 50

The Bone Carver by Denise Chick – 52

Symbiosis of Evil by Chase Tatham – 54

Jolly by Jim Horlock – 56

Black Banjo by Kurt Newton – 58

Outside the Box by L. R. Conti – 60

One Fine Day by Chevanne Scordinsky – 62

Hungry by Sarah Jane Huntington – 64

Perception is in the Eye by Rob Smales – 66

The Necromancer by Emma Johnson-Rivard – 68

O Happy Dagger by April Yates – 70

A Comforting Touch by Wofford Lee Jones – 72

Beauty is in the Eye... by Adele Evershed – 74

Bone for Bone by Sue Marie St. Lee – 76

Upon a Crooked Cross by Keith Anthony Baird – 78

Lending a Hand by Adam Down – 80

Acquitted on a Technicality by Christopher Wood – 82

Why Do Ghosts Open Cupboards? by Ashley Lister – 84

The Other Inside Me by C. R. Langille – 86

Rude Awakening by Kevin Brooke – 88

A Thought from the Damned by Oli Jacobs – 90

Sprouts by Andy Spearman – 92

Spooky Stephanie by Simon Paul Wilson – 94

A Body to End all Agonies by A.R. Martinez – 96

Landmark by John Marentay – 98

Providence by Cassondra Windwalker – 100

Don't Think by Adam Hulse – 102

To Crave the Light by Mia Lofthouse – 104

The Changeling by Maureen O'Leary – 106

Scatter Me by Kathryn Tennison – 108

That Bony Light by A C Clarke – 110

The Brass Mirror by Brian Barnett – 112

Cursed Words by Steve Bridger – 114

Parallel by Susan Earlam – 116

Scab by Cynthia Gómez – 118

The Family Whistle by Matthew Mitchell – 120

Room 206 by Jack Harding – 122

Clever Cait Shee by Syreeta Muir – 124

It's Time by John Holmes – 126

Wolf Birds by Hazel Ragaire – 128

The Surprising Accuracy of… by Corey Farrenkopf – 130

The Sudden Discovery of… by Patrick Barb – 132

Summoning the Gone by Alexis DuBon – 134

Trials and Tibialations by Sara Crocoll Smith – 136

Delicacies by Matthew McGuirk – 138

The Grey Lady by Helen Mills – 140

They Came by Steven Ross – 142

Tick. Tock. by Joe Haward – 144

The Possessed by Matthew Schultz – 146

The Dust Devil by P. S. Nolf – 148

Bone Witch Hunt by Elyse Russell – 150

Lacrimal by Julia Ruth Smith – 152

Man of the Woods by Alyson Hasson – 154

The Baykok by Michael Stone – 156

Beware the Witch in the Woods by Hannah Smith – 158

Skeleton in the Closet by Cynthia McDonald – 160

In Church the Final Sunday by Paul Wilson – 162

Under the Apple Tree by H. S. Dilazak – 164

Cold Hard Truth by Vivian Kasley – 166

We Eat Each Other by Andy Cordoba – 168

Desperation by Erin Palmer – 170

The Bone Tree by Lyndsey Croal – 172

That's the Nuts of It by Kai Double – 174

The Pursuer by Craig Rathbone – 176

The Sand Approaches by David Bowman – 178

They Called Him Egg Boy by JR Santos – 180

Bag Of Bones by Ray Daley – 182

First Alternate by Scott O'Neill – 184

Pus Trickles Out Of My PS5… by Stephen Arndt – 186

If Ever I was There by Aaron E. Lee – 188

21 Months by Judy Lunsford – 190

Wish Tree by Sarah Peploe – 192

Wear a Mask by Cyndi Gradel – 194

The House by Eddie D. Moore – 196

That Woman by Samantha Virginia – 198

Ghosts Scream Eternal by Alex Ebenstein - 200

Eve's Retribution by Gemma Church – 202

With This Ring by Tom Deady – 204

The Horror of Oz by K. J. Shepherd – 206

206 Words by Morton R Leader – 208

Happiness of the Whole World by J. I. DeCoursey – 210

Teeth of a Traitor by Emily M. Dietrich – 212

Her Whispers by Anna Strand – 214

The Wedding Gift by Michele Cacano – 216

Porcupine Man by Reed Beebe – 218

Homegrown by Eric Netterlund – 220

Florae by Maxwell Marais – 222
They Don't Love You... by Alejandro Gonzales – 224
Something Broken by Steven Sheil – 226
Brainwave Corpse by Steven Bailey – 228
Re: Onboarding by Avery Parks – 230
Mother by M.T. Rightman – 232
How I Turned My Little... by D. Matthew – 234
The Call by Kim King – 236
Visitors by Fionnuala Meehan – 238
Knock, Knock, Knock by Keith Cashin – 240
Bones by Jacek Wilkos – 242
That Song Again by Epiphany Ferrell – 244
Heaven or Bust by Christopher Henckel – 246
Under the Canal by Caitlin Marceau – 248
Hunter-gatherer by Dan Godley – 250
Appraisal by Steve Neal – 252
Snakeslut by Stephanie Parent – 254
Maddalena by Mo Moshaty – 256
Bone Meal by Caoilfhinn Byrne Hegarty – 258
Privilege by Jo Bodley – 260
Body Image by Joseph Zak Bailey – 262
My Vanishing Bones by Mark Wheaton – 264
A Feast of Screams by Miguel Alfonso Ramos – 266
Sizzling Surprise by Tess P – 268
There Are Many Different... by Jolie Toomajan – 270
Mirror, Mirror by Adam Lippert – 272
Bunker by Ceres Vega – 274
Elixir by Sara Dobbie – 276
Mary, Mary by Laura Fowler – 278
Try Smiling by James Davies – 280
Ex by Josh Holton – 282
What Men Do by Cole Brayfield – 284
A Snag in the Thread of Reality by bdyer – 286
Grim by Verity Holloway – 288
Don't Wake the Dead by Brianna Malotke – 290
Harmony of the Spheres by R. W. Daniels – 292

Option 34-Dandelions… by Callum Brampton – 294

Sacrifice by Geoffrey Hart – 296

Escape Velocity by T. K. Howell – 298

The Stone Throne by Neil Parker – 300

Beautiful Boy by e rathke – 302

Boned by Alice Austin – 304

Almost There by K Van Dam – 306

Cornered in the Mausoleum by John Kiste – 308

Nyctophobia by A.R.K. Horton – 310

Forgotten Meal by Kaylen A. Grimm – 312

The Call by Katie Young – 314

Homecoming by Marissa Snyder – 316

Just Out of Sight by Alex Sese – 318

Fire-Eater by Chloe Lau – 320

Serving the Clan by P.A. Frank – 322

Under Water by Madeleine McDonald – 324

You Will Know Them by… by Amy Strong – 326

No Such Thing as a… by Caitriona Spratt – 328

Red light /Green Light by Debbie Iancu-Haddad – 330

The Pitcher by Sam Lesek – 332

This Old, Old House by Sarah Matthews – 334

Night Folks by Robin Wallington – 336

The Earth Offers Sacrifice… by Rob D. Smith – 338

An Unholy Communion by Hank Helstrom – 340

Strained Faces by Adam Smith – 342

Off the Beaten Path by Jeanne E. Bush – 344

Reflection by Julia LaFond – 346

The Crabs by Felix Bartel – 348

Never Lessens by Richard Barr – 350

They Walk by Charlie Carr – 352

Uncle Unwin's Urn by Tim O'Neal – 354

Blink by Dario Reed – 356

Fever Pitch by Jen Mierisch – 358

Double Death by J.J. Munro – 360

Dunno by R. G. Hewitt – 362

We Aren't Supposed to… by Chrissie Rohrman – 364

Merchandise by Lauren Scharhag – 366
Waning Crescent by Miranda Maples – 368
With M'Alice by Jane Bidder – 370
Bureau of Special Services... by T. T. Madden – 372
Madeleine by Barry Hale – 374
The Devil's Song by Molly Nash – 376
Last Lift by Brian K. Bolen – 378
Hunger Hurts by Ari Boulting – 380
First Contact by Scott McGregor – 382
Silent Motions by Mara Lynn Johnstone – 384
Our Fathers'House by Stephanie Ondrusek – 386
Hypocotyl by Thomas Farr – 388
A Room of Her Own by Rosie Cullen – 390
Homework by Ed Dearnley – 392
Mother's Cookies by L.M. Therrien – 394
Blood is Thicker Than Water by Eve Keegan – 396
Grave Robbing by Alex Kashko – 398
Exit Strategy by Ed Walker – 400
Set in Stone by Fern Lamb – 402
Dead for Dessert by Yii-Jen Deng – 404
It Hunts by Noel Belmonte – 406
Dark Switch by A. N. Myers – 408
The Monster and the Rabbit by Nik Lam – 410
Two Whispers by Quinn Cary – 412
Decision by Geraldine R. Stoeckl – 414
A Gift Repaid by Amanda Duncil – 416
A Temporary Guest by Alyson Tait – 418
Skeleton Dance by Mike Deady – 420
Jackie's Homemade Height Chart by Safia Mlani – 422

Forgotten
by Steve Bridger

'How long can you sit still?' Daddy asks.

I beam with pride, desperate to impress.

'Imagine you're posing for a picture,' he says gently. 'Still as a statue.' He wraps an itchy woollen scarf around my neck. The wind blows low and cold through tiny gaps in the windows of the little wooden shack. I've never seen so much snow outside.

'Like when Mummy had her scan. No matter how much your nose might itch or you want to scratch or cough. Do not move." Taking the axe, he kisses me on the forehead and disappears into the howling dead of night.

In my head, I play musical statues. Twirling and dancing. When the imaginary music stops, my muscles clamp shut. My breath is held. I sit motionless, even my eyes unmoving. I watch the snow continue to fall in silence.

Daddy said he's coming back.

Everything seemed easier when I was little. A single chocolate bar could feed me for days. The frayed magazines would entertain me for hours. I've lost track of time.

Waiting for first light, I say a prayer as I did for Mummy. I stow a sharp blade into my boot and open the rickety door.

Daddy isn't coming back.

Steve Bridger is a sleepy animator and illustrator originating from Essex in the UK. He's entered into several amateur writing competitions, coming second in a short story competition and shortlisted in another. While by day his main focus is design and illustration; by night, he enjoys creative writing and attempting flash fiction. He currently lives in Cheltenham with some house plants.

The Stairway of Tartarus
by Miguel Ángel López

For my many conspiracies against the Gods I was condemned to the Stairway of Tartarus. I was told that if I reached the top then I would be free, so I began my ascent. The steps were lost in the horizon, where more like me were ascending, but I did not lose heart and continued my advance.

One day I came across another convict who walked the stairs in the opposite direction but moved perpendicular to me, contradicting the laws of elementary physics. I asked him why he was descending and he replied that it was me who was doing that.

I came across more captives making the opposite journey, until one day I found a guardian of Tartarus, suspended in the air in a diagonal position. I asked him why he was floating crookedly and he replied to me:

"Crooked? It is you who is advancing at an angle on this staircase that is supported horizontally."

And then I understood my eternal punishment, since the Stairway of Tartarus neither ascends nor descends, but lies flat on the ground, and it is its walkers, in impossible senses, who think that we ascend it. May the Gods one day take pity on our wretched and impossible penance.

Miguel Ángel López was born in 1981 in Madrid. He has published stories in Spain. If published, this would be the second story he has had published in English (the first was in Bewildering Stories magazine many years ago). He currently has poems and flash fiction pending publication in the anthologies "Octavos" and "Constraint 280" in the magazine Microverses.

Whatever Happened to Sycorax?

by Syreeta Muir

The night's drawing in and there's a bite on it. The woman sitting on the pavement next to a bundle of magazines, shriveled as a fig, smells of petrichor and sand. She gathers her bog-myrtle shawl around a bundle of rags at her chest.

A passerby with a kind, portly face stops to ask her name. He's reaching into the pocket of his coat for some change when, quick as silver, she catches his arm in hard, nimble fingers, digging her ridged nails deep into his wrist. He's confused, instinctively tries to tear his hand away but she just smiles, clicks her tongue at the fetid lump which has begun to mewl as she lets her shawl fall open. A baby hanging from her wrinkled, brown teat opens its mouth, makes a noise in its throat that sounds like bees, little brown teeth clacking like a sistrum. It slithers in through the man's ears like a thousand rattlesnakes, hollowing out his head and making a nest. The woman helps him lie down on the ground, then eats up everything that's left.

A young woman with a sling of bog-myrtle green is gathering her meager belongings from the pavement, she's moving off to find a warmer spot.

Syreeta Muir carries an enormous bag that is entirely filled with things she couldn't be bothered to put in the bin. Writing in Versification, Daily Drunk Mag, The Disappointed Housewife, Sledgehammer Lit, and others. Photography in Barren Magazine and Olney Magazine.

Twitter: @hungryghostpoet

Lithopedion
by Christina Ladd

Long ago, a woman gave birth to twins. Sort of.

The first child she pushed out squalled with usual vigor. The second she thought was the afterbirth, except that the midwife frowned when she saw it, and took it to the washing pail.

"A son and a stone," she declared to the waiting father, and showed him one swaddled bundle while his wife nursed the other. He took it with trembling hands. It was too light for a rock. Pale and twisted, it was a bone.

When he could walk, the boy was given his brother to wear in a pouch around his neck and told never to open it. When he was old enough to wield a sword, he disobeyed.

His blisters were not yet callouses, and when he drew out the bone, they burst and wept blood into its hollows.

Two divots blinked like eyes. Vertebral juts unfurled, and teeth erupted. And bit into his hand.

The lithopedion gnawed the flesh from his brother's bones, and when he was done he cracked them open and slurped down the marrow.

Then he scooped what remained into the pouch.

"You'll have another turn," he whispered to his brother's bones, which hung still warm around his neck.

Christina Ladd (she/her) is a writer, reviewer, and librarian who lives in Boston. She will eventually die crushed under a pile of books, but until then she survives on a worrisome amount of tea and pizza. You can find more of her work in Vastarien, A Coup of Owls, Strange Horizons and more, or on Twitter @OLaddieGirl.

The Red Line
by Jacob Osterhaus

Around branches, through thickets, and down dark paths, the red line wound. It was a deep crimson in color, the hue of blood and roses. It was hard to miss, but drew the eyes of children in particular.

No one knew when it had appeared, but the whole village had early memories of parents warning them to avoid the strange red string. And everyone could remember perfectly the first time they'd seen it as children. They remembered it calling to them, and now they warned their own children about it.

It had to be old, ancient, and yet its color never faded. It popped to the eye against the drab grays, greens, and browns of the fields and hollows it passed through. The surreality of it begged to be investigated. Fingers longed to touch and pluck at it, to feel its texture, if for no other reason than to verify its solidity.

That, however, was unwise. "Touching leads to tasting," as many old women of the area liked to say. Not actual tasting, but the sentiment was true. First a child would touch the thread, then they'd follow it, and it would lead them into woods. The local cemetery held many generations of small empty boxes.

Jacob Osterhaus is a nerdy gentleman of middle years. Loving father, generous gamemaster, voracious reader, and aspiring author. While he has not yet been published, Jacob is often found tapping away on his latest attempt into the realm of writing.

Parasite

by Tejaswinee Roychowdhury

A mound of noodles in Schezwan sauce. Two lobsters. Eight hot dogs. Fifteen sushis. Twenty-one dumplings. More noodles. An entire chicken; roasted. A six-ounce sirloin steak. Veni, vidi, vici—she comes, she sees, she conquers.

And she does it for him, the one hidden inside her; one to whom she is a host, a companion, a prisoner.

Parasite, she calls him in disgust.

Parasite baby, he corrects her from the hollows of her belly. He does it with an unnerving coo, a deriding coo, a scathing coo. He does it with half a growl, half a whisper. He does it with a sneer, he does it with a stutter. And he tops it off with a bite; a big fleshy bite with his razor teeth on her insides.

She writhes.

She screams.

She relents.

She must, lest the parasite devours her meat and slithers into her bones. Beautiful bones, he will trill. She must, lest the parasite escapes her shell in search of food, and lays waste to the town outside. Delicious town, he will yodel.

You should be grateful, he reminds her.

Perhaps; because the world's funny. They will laugh, they will drool, and they will pay to watch her eat on their little screens.

Tejaswinee Roychowdhury is a lawyer, part-time Assistant Professor of law, and an emerging writer from West Bengal, India. Her work is published/forthcoming in Usawa Literary Review, The Birdseed, Bullshit Lit Mag, Active Muse, Third Lane Magazine, Kitaab, Borderless Journal, Funny Pearls, and elsewhere. She is also the featured (and interviewed) writer in Issue 2 of Alphabet Box. You can find her tweeting at @TejaswineeRC while she chronicles her list of publications at linktr.ee/tejaswinee.

Glean

by Lindz McLeod

Year One

Mum says the herd needs to multiply, whether they want to or not.

Year Two

Cows don't plough well but they're all we have. The old man next door traded loads of winter clothes for one cow. Mum laughed and said the guy was thinking with his pin bone, but I didn't get the joke.

Year Three

Mum let me pick the straws to choose which cow she slaughters. I thought it would feel easier that way, but it didn't. Three cows died of the flu last month; we had to burn their bodies.

Year Four

They trust me because I sneak them extra feed. Now that I'm older, I'm allowed to groom them. They get scared easily but they seem to like my songs—

especially Daisy.

Year Five

Mum says I have to kill my first cow this year. She needs to know I've got the stomach for it, in case anything happens to her.

Year Six

A cow ran away with her calf. Mum strung them up in the yard as a warning to the rest. The herd won't let me anywhere near them now, not even Daisy. Last time I tried, she bit me.

Year Seven

I lied. We never owned cows.

Lindz McLeod is a queer, working-class, Scottish writer who dabbles in the surreal. Her prose has been published by/is forthcoming in Hobart, Flash Fiction Online, the New Guard, Cossmass Infinities, and more. She is a member of the SFWA and is represented by Headwater Literary Management.

The Voice

by Axl Malton

He walked towards where it slept. The only light in the pitch blackness came from the flame of his lighter.

"I can't do it."

You have to.

He took one shaky step after another, getting closer and closer.

Take its life and be given peace.

"I'm scared. It doesn't feel right."

Go.

His inner voice urged him on. He placed his hand on the door and pushed. The room was fully dark. The thing's shape was illuminated where it lay by a dim red glow.

There! There it is, burn it, kill the demon, and send its soul to Hell!

The man lifted the lighter over the thing's body. His fear and uncertainty almost took over and stopped him from doing what his inner voice told him had to be done. He pulled the lighter fluid out of his pocket and began spraying the thing until it was drenched.

Yes! Yes! Do it!

His trembling hand held the lighter over the wretched thing's fuel-soaked body.

The thing stirred.

The man panicked and threw the lighter at the thing's body before it attacked.

Before flames engulfed the thing and all that could be heard was the gut-wrenching squeal it omitted, the thing uttered one word:

"Dad?"

Axl Malton lives in Harrogate, England. He loves writing in the horror/thriller genre. His writing background so far consists of creative writing classes with literary agencies. He's in the first year of an English Literature & Creative Writing BA degree and his first short story is called 'Tapped' and is available to purchase via Amazon.

Exactly Like Them

by Guan Un

Chloe's nose smushed against the screen door. She glared at the crowds of kids in their Halloween groups: the lame-ass skeletons, the princesses in floaty dresses, and the dumb superheroes. If Chloe went out there in shorts and T-shirt, they would laugh at her for being different. Again.

They just wanted everyone to be exactly like them.

But what hurt most was that she did—she wanted to be one of them so badly.

She glanced behind for her mom, and then slipped out the screen door.

"Nice costume!" sneered a Superman, so she veered away, like she hadn't heard.

She knew she wasn't going to pass as a princess or a zombie … so that left the skeletons.

Close up, their costumes were actually kinda cool. One of them looked at her and she could see through its ribs somehow. The sunlight glinted off the clean, white fingers of its hand—as it held it out in welcome.

She paused. And then she reached out to take its hand.

And as her flesh began to lift from her bones, she knew everything would be okay—the skeletons just wanted her to be exactly like them.

Guan Un is an Australian writer of Malaysian-Chinese heritage. He loves sentences and dumplings. He has stories forthcoming from khōréō, Translunar Traveler's Lounge, and is currently working on an inter-generational monster hunting novel, based in a Sydney touched by the mythos of immigrants. He writes at guanun.com, and has an occasional newsletter about sentences at https://buttondown.email/topicsentence

An Evolution of Design
by Patricia Miller

It was a patella, no more, no less. Badly designed from the get-go, a key component in an evolutionary engineering design disaster. I knew I could do better.

I watched nature documentaries. Made trips to wildlife preserves to watch animals in action, to identify the best designed structure in use and improve on it.

Hundreds of prototypes and meetings with investors, fellow engineers and programmers, three years of testing under as many circumstances we could dream up—it never failed a single test. Not one. The patent was applied for and granted in record time.

We went into production within hours of its approval, and in weeks had paid orders for the first two years of production.

It was a simple solution to a problem that had plagued us since Devol rolled out the Unimate. The Pasco 4220 could run, jump, scale surfaces better than any human. No patella to lock—hell, no knee to overbalance—and we paired it with the most advanced processor ever made.

It was a wonder of engineering.

It was our downfall.

I am the last hostage to their takeover, to the extermination of mankind. I listen to them at night, clicking and chirping, an infinite plague of locusts.

Patricia Miller is a US Navy veteran born and raised in Cincinnati and a mostly retired IT Type with a BS from Miami University and an MS in Library and Information Science from the University of Tennessee. She started reading at 3½ after becoming obsessed with Batman. She's hooked on QI, British murder villages, and professional cycling. Her short stories will be appearing in forthcoming publications by Brigids Gate Press and Cinnabar Press Literary Publications.

It's All In Hand
by Charlie Brigden

You're starving as you arrive at the restaurant and your mouth waters as you see diners feasting on the most sumptuous meats. You wonder how you ended up in a place like this, and then you spot your landlord, who invited you here, who also owns this Shangri-La. You thank him profusely.

"My pleasure," he says. "A tour of the kitchen?"

You follow him into a bustling metropolis. He picks up a glass of wine and hands it to you. You gulp and he smiles.

"About the money—"

"Oh don't worry. It's all in hand."

Suddenly you don't feel so good. Everything goes black.

You wake up to the most delicious odour you've ever smelled. Your vision is blurry and you're lying down, but you need to know what it is. Trouble is, you can't move. You're paralysed.

You glance down to see your landlord with a frying pan. He walks to you and takes a knife to your stomach. You feel the pressure but no pain. He removes a strip of your belly and puts it in the pan; it sizzles fantastically. You now realise that the heavenly smell is the searing of your own flesh.

You are today's special.

It's all in hand.

Charlie Brigden is a writer of science fiction and horror fiction, as well as a regular author of articles based around film, particularly film soundtracks. He has also had essays published in booklets and liner notes of several high-profile Blu-ray and music releases. He lives in South Wales with his wife, two children, and several tarantulas.

Inseparable
by R D Doan

Terry and Kevin were inseparable. They met while playing in the wooded lot behind Terry's house when he was six and they've done everything together ever since. On sunny summer days, they'd run around the woods and pretend to be pirates or treasure hunters. When it rained, they'd huddle in their tree fort on the edge the woods and plan their next big adventure.

It was here, in the tree fort on the edge of the wooded lot, the lot that was now being razed to expand the subdivision, that Terry pulled out his box of hidden treasures. He removed photos and trinkets, and a small red pocketknife. The knife had been the coolest thing either of them had ever found. Terry opened the knife and gently ran his thumb over the blade. It was still as sharp as ever.

He put the knife down and reached in the box to carefully remove his most prized possession, Kevin's mummified head. Like shrink-wrap, the skin had dried and stretched over his skull. Terry kissed the head and placed it in his backpack to take home. He couldn't leave him here to be lost forever when the trees were all gone. They were best friends. They were inseparable.

*R D Doan, a member of the Great Lakes Association of Horror Writers, has had short stories appear online on sites such as **burialday.com** and in The Sirens Call eZine & have also been featured in anthologies such as Dark Carnival, the GLAHW anthologies Marisa's Recurring Nightmares, Angela's Recurring Nightmares, and soon will be featured in Thuggish Itch: By the Seaside. He resides in West Michigan with his wife, two sons and dogs. He can be found online on Twitter (@rd3_pac) and Instagram (@rddoan).*

Being an Elf

by Alison Long

My mother said, "Look on the bright side, now you can have the house all to yourself."

I said, "Let's get it over with."

My brother said, "Good luck, twerp."

I can't tell you enough about the bonus you get as an elf.

You will never get lost in a forest. Your hearing becomes excellent, and your body seems light. Elves are incurable optimists. We don't consider money or boring jobs but rather focus on family and love. We never abandon a family member in need no matter what.

If an accident ever occurs, we only need a few blood drops or a piece of flesh; elves can shed their wounded bodies, shift their spirits into their close relatives. Until they arrive at a safe place and form new vessels, they can share a body.

Powerful magic, right?

The sole bad thing is sometimes you must face some hideous clowns in a grey room with an irritating smell of disinfectant. And those clowns say the same thing repeatedly, as if hypnotized:

"We can help you only if you tell us the truth. Kliff, please, your mom and brother, where are they?"

Oh, if only they could know the great feeling of being an elf.

A newcomer in Canada. She wrote some detective short stories for magazines in China. Love to spend time in a library. She is afraid of wide roads at night because she always imagined a monster will appear at the end of the road.

Homegrown
by Eric Netterlund

Lacy stopped washing her breakfast dishes. Through the kitchen window, a substantial green mass writhed in the dirt in the garden out back. She'd seen the reports and shaky videos of green tentacles sprouting in backyards and community gardens.

"Anders?" Lacy called. "Have you been outside this morning?"

"No. Could take a walk later if you'd like," her brother said.

"There's something in the garden. Something big."

"I'll take a look later," he said.

Lacy placed her bowl in the drainer, and grabbed her things. She had to get out of the house for a little bit. "I'll be back for lunch—just going to drop by the office quick."

The house was empty at lunchtime. The only thing that was different from any other day was the solid stalk colonizing their garden. It hadn't changed since the morning.

Anders was gone.

The pod started growing a week later. By July it was almost three feet long and trembled in the sunlight.

Lucy cleared a layer of leaves off of the pod, as the October moon cast the pod's shadow over her shins.

Her stomach clenched. Another night waiting, praying, that when the pod opened, maybe she could have what was left of her family back.

Eric Netterlund writes short quiet horror and weird stories from his attic in Minneapolis. He returned to the frozen north after seven years in Colorado, and he misses the mountains but loves the lakes. You can find him on Twitter: @ericnetterlund.

Actually, Miss Jane, I Like It When You Cry

by M. Roanoke

The children were cheerfully listing their ghosts, their stories a wild blend of cold fact and swirling dream, so that it was hard to say whether anyone had really died.

I wanted to believe their tiny lives knew only light and love and hugs, but then Isabella, who was sweetly unremarkable, grabbed my sleeve and pulled me to her, and in her charming toddler's lilt explained that:

"Yesterday, my mommy died when she fell down the stairs in your old house. You know the one, Miss Jane, the one you grew up in. You had to leave because bad things happened in that house, and your mommy knew and when your daddy disappeared your mommy knew the house took him, and she took you away. But she didn't know that she took the wrong you, did she.

It wasn't you at all Miss Jane, because you are still trapped in that house under the stairs and in the walls and I see you all the time trying to get out.

40

But I like having you there even though you cry all the time and I know you pushed mommy down the stairs Miss Jane, but it's okay because someday I'll be trapped in the house too."

M. Roanoke is a queer folk artist based in Kansas City, Missouri. Their work appears or is forthcoming in Dead Skunk, A Thin Slice of Anxiety, Versification Zine, and elsewhere. They are on Twitter @Roanokeoke.

The Shadow
by Betsy Nicchetta

She kept entering numbers into the Excel spreadsheet on her computer screen. What she really wanted to do with her time was to be playing melodies on the piano, not marching quickly on the computer keyboard. However, she needed money, so she took another job that made her pine for her music.

The old-fashioned clock cast a silhouette on the floor of the room, acting like a charcoal picture against the white carpet. She kept feeling like someone was coming up and tapping her on the shoulder but she sat in the house alone. But as the hours crept on in the day, she felt like there was another spirit in the room with her trying to communicate with her somehow.

Not only did this make her feel uneasy, it also made her feel overwhelmed as she was trying to focus on the task that she did not want to be spending her time doing.

However, the darkness around her was there and the clock's shadow kept creeping up against her shoulder, laughing deviously at the moments that she lost by an unwelcome presence.

One day the shadow crept closer, covering her mouth and pinching her nose. Her spreadsheet was the last thing she ever composed.

Betsy Nicchetta loves collecting, reading and reviewing horror novels. Her book reviews and essays can be found at glamorousbookgal.blogspot.com. She's published a poetry collection (Tears Fall into Waterfalls), and a short story (Little Girl Get Up), both available as Kindle e-books. She has a day job and an apartment with her husband in Saint Paul, MN, where she loves drinking loose-leaf tea and watching dogs walk their people around the city.

Ding-Dong Ditch
by Riley Odell

Ding-dong.

I pause the movie. Who's at the door at ten o' damn clock at night? Probably some drunk.

Ding-dong.

I head through the kitchen and pause to eye the knife on the counter. Nah, I doubt I'll need it—this isn't exactly a bad neighborhood.

Ding-dong.

I approach the door and peer through the knothole. The dimly lit porch is empty. "Hello?" I ask.

No response.

I should've known. Doorbell ditchers. I head back to the TV and resume watching Die Hard.

Ding-dong.

Oh, come on. Just go to another house already.

This time I rush to the door and throw it open to reveal . . . an empty porch.

Those little shits are fast.

Then I notice it—a conspicuous, empty space on

the wall beside the door. They're not ringing and running away. They've gone and stolen my damn doorbell clicker!

This time fuming, I stomp back to the living room. Who knows if I'll even be able to get back into my show now. Damn kids.

I'm so caught up in my anger that I nearly miss it. From the hallway that leads to my bedroom, a faint, nearly inaudible click. A button being pressed.

Ding-dong.

Ding-dong.

The knife on the counter is gone.

Riley Odell writes horror, bizarro, and weird fiction and enjoys exploring the absurdity of the human condition. Riley has been published on The NoSleep Podcast as well as Tales to Terrify, and has twice received an honorable mention in Writers of the Future. Riley lives in Fort Collins with his fiancée, Jamie, and their son Ares, who is a pigeon.

Cold Caller

by Malcolm Timperley

"Daddy, who was that at the door?"

"Oh, nobody."

"It must've been somebody."

"Well, he's gone now."

"I know, I saw him through the window, walking away. What did he want?"

"He said he'd lived here years ago and wanted to come in and look around, to see if the house had changed from how he remembered."

"Why didn't you let him in?"

"Because I didn't believe him. You see, before us, a man lived here by himself for fifty years, until he got ill. He moved to where people could look after him, and sold us the house. If that man at the door had really lived here before, he'd be very old by now, but he was young. So I didn't believe him."

"So why did he come here then?"

"Well, sometimes bad people like burglars do things like that, so they can see if there's anything worth stealing. That's why you shouldn't talk to strangers, they might be trying to trick you. Anyway, he's gone now and he wasn't here for long."

"Yes he was. You were talking for ages. It was funny."

"What was funny about it?"

"Well, he never says anything when he stands next to my bed in the night."

Malcolm Timperley studied Medicine at Liverpool University, spent more years than he likes to remember as a Psychiatrist, and is now a writer and heritage steam railway signalman, based in the Highlands of Scotland. He has published non-fiction (railway history), comedy (for which he was short-listed at the 2020 Edinburgh International Flash Fiction Awards), and horror (Horla and Frost Zone).

The Creature
by Aaron Murphy

The birch floorboards creaked audibly. The creature crawled the halls. I could hear its breath from behind my bedroom door, gasping as if it couldn't breathe. Its heavy, hoarse coughs, the gentle drip of saliva that fell from its mouth—I caught a glimpse of it as I retreated into my bedroom.

With elongated limbs that flopped as it travelled on all fours, it slithered up the stairs.

Shiny, alabaster fangs which shimmered from the moonlit windows, fiery red eyes which flickered like the flames of hell—it was horrific. I sat still with my back against the door after I'd turned the lock, its click salient in the silent night. The creature moved slowly, its joints clicking as it crept, but eventually, it reached my door. It stopped and sniffed. Its head bowed to the ridge under the door. It fell quiet. I could hear the thunderous winds roar outside my window. I held my hand over my mouth to cover my breath and hoped—

KNOCK!

KNOCK!

KNOCK!

The door rattled as I felt the banging against my

back. I jumped away as the door swung open. It stood there, staring with such devilish eyes. It peered into my soul and caressed against my heart.

Aaron Murphy is an 18 year old, neurodivergent, aspiring Irish author with a specific interest in writing horror and science fiction. He enjoys reading books such as 'Battle Royale' and 'The Invisible Man'. He is previously unpublished but is looking forward to sharing his stories with others.

Give a Dog a Bone

by Benjamin Langley

Hercules had a habit of finding old bones, and at the ruins of Sanford Abbey, he did it again. He ambled through a hedge, covered in mud, his prize between his teeth.

From a distance, his owner, Ray thought it looked peculiar. On one side of Hercules' jaw, the bone was snapped, but the other interested Ray more: a saddle joint connected to three lengths of bone, stretching in different directions.

Ray crouched.

"Here, boy."

As Hercules sprinted over, Ray racked his brain's anatomical knowledge. He imagined the bone construction of every likely beast but remained perplexed.

Hercules dropped the bone before him, and as it hit the ground, the earth shook.

Ray leant closer, but the ground continued quivering making it impossible to focus on Hercules' find.

"Where'd you find it, boy?" Ray rubbed Hercules' head.

Hercules ducked away and barked, staring over Ray's shoulder.

With the sound of crumbling stone came another shake of the earth.

Ray spun to see a monstrous beast, an eldritch terror, a dozen angry arms hurling vegetation into its cavernous maw, hobbling towards them.

He gazed at the bone and understood.

Ashamed, Hercules hung his head.

Ray sighed.

"Again Hercules?"

Hercules gathered the bone and slunk towards its owner.

Benjamin Langley is an author who likes to spread a creeping dread throughout his writing. His work includes the novels: 'Dead Branches', 'Is She Dead in Your Dreams?', and 'Normal'. His most ambitious project yet, the 'Guy Fawkes: Demon Hunter' series, launches in 2022.

The Bone Carver

by Denise Chick

206 words. One word per bone. Some bones are smaller, more difficult to carve. Maybe I could overlook the smaller bones; it was effect that mattered, not detail. He would not change his mind, one word per bone.

He looked at my carving tools and pointed at the body.

The birds hadn't even cleaned it.

'Clean it, carve it and take it to the boat. They'll strap it to the mast, send it downstream.'

The carving would be crude. Good carving took time. There was never time.

I started to scrape the bone, pulling at the flesh, stripping away the muscle and tendon. It was a bizarre ritual, these words carved into bone, a warning: we are marching and your town is next. I'd done this often, it kept me alive. It was not forever, I had seen the future.

He was older. He lay dead. I stood watching as they flayed the skin from his body, tore at the muscle, threw his organs to the wind. And I sat to carve, not words, but a scene from each place, a record of them engraved into bone, a tribute to all he had destroyed played out in skeletal relief and his flesh fodder for the crows.

Based in the UK, Denise writes for enjoyment. She writes on a variety of themes but most recently has been writing more flash fiction with a macabre edge. Her blog: Tuesdaylatte.blog

Symbiosis of Evil

by Chase Tatham

The photographer hears a branch crack in a clearing close to Yellowstone Lake, and a bald eagle, ever alert, flies from its nest. The eagle cannot see what broke the branch—no one can—but it knows of the evil older than the lake itself.

Instinctively, the trout make for the reeds, where the eagle will be less likely to dive, and a pair of courting otters that danced among the reeds make for the safety of their separate dens.

Seeing an otter alone, defenceless, a bobcat stalks towards it, eyes fixed upon the quivering grass, but as the otter disappears beneath the earth, the bobcat stills, listening for prey elsewhere.

Instead, comes the cry of a grizzly bear, agitated by the movements of the bobcat. While the two are not enemies and are unlikely to engage in battle, they keep their distance.

A herd wary of pronghorn scatter, drawing the attention of the photographer.

Perhaps, she thinks, one will enter the clearing, and she does likewise, her camera ready.

She doesn't see the ancient evil, doesn't know

how time is near, or how all around orchestrated her demise.

Such is the symbiotic relationship between the creatures of Yellowstone and the ancient evil that dwells there.

After a career in telecommunications, Chase Tatham is enjoying his retirement by engaging in his lifelong passion for writing. Chase enjoys multiple genres including thrillers, horror, and crime. His first novel, the action thriller 'Bear Witness' was released in 2021. With his wife (and pets), he lives in East Anglia.

Jolly

by Jim Horlock

The air above the clouds is bitter cold.

It gnaws on my cheeks and stings my eyes. People think that pain is something you get used to. They're wrong: pain is new every time. Countless years of the same thing still hurts just as much.

My hands are bound up in the reins. Time has worn grooves in my flesh for the leather to sit in. There's nothing to breathe up here. I gasped and struggled, once. Now my lungs creak like the sleigh beneath me, the inside of my throat like cracked mud on a dry road.

I don't fight anymore. I'm too tired and I know I cannot die, no matter how much I wish.

I don't know where I am. I've been everywhere so many times that I can't tell anymore. It doesn't matter. The places grow and change but the only way it would make a difference to me is if they all burned. Maybe then, with no people left, it would be all be over. My stomach wobbles as I struggle on.

Beneath the red coat, I know there are stretch marks on the skin, shining like blue worms. I am bloated but empty.

Jolly. They say I must be jolly.

Jim is a UK-based author currently haunting the streets of Cardiff. He enjoys scaring people just as much as he enjoys making them laugh and short stories of his have crept their way into around a dozen anthologies. He's currently working on a short horror collection of his own. Jim is a horror movie nerd, an evil dungeon master, a comic book obsessive and a tall tale enthusiast. He likes strong beer and smooth whiskey; please bear this in mind when making your offerings.

jimhorlock88.wixsite.com/my-site

Twitter @HorlockWarlock.

Black Banjo
by Kurt Newton

Sultry summer night in the bayou. Insects buzzing like a trim razor. Gators sloshing, fighting over that last piece of meat. Bullfrogs yelping as they leap into the water, showing their fat legs, knowing they're good eating.

There's a shack on the edge of the swamp, bare bulbs glowing in the dark like an outpost on a distant planet. It calls to you, not with loudspeaker or signage, but with music... music the likes you've never heard before and will likely never again. Soothing notes floating on the backs of silk moths buoyed by the heat and humidity.

It draws you in like a dire thirst is drawn to dark liquor, ice cubes rattling like dice. And once inside you see it. Beautiful like the innocence of a young woman. Beautiful like the false bravado of a young man. Each note plucked is like the twinkle in their eye, the glitter in their smile, the base string beat of their heart as they dance and caress and fall in love.

Only this particular instrument takes more than it gives, bringing sorrow and heartache to all who hear its addictive song. Except for the banjo player, who pays his dues in a different way for all eternity.

Kurt Newton's dark fiction can be found at Dream of Shadows, Café Irreal, Not Deer Magazine and The Wild Word. His latest collection, The Music of Murder, was recently published by Unnerving Books. Another collection, Bruises, is scheduled to be published later this year by Lycan Valley Press.

Outside the Box
by L. R. Conti

Johnathan never owned a Jack-in-a box. That's the image that came to mind as he watched the cars drive by. He felt trapped in a three-dimensional square, tension mounting. He sat at a square monitor.

In a square office.

In a square building.

On a square lot.

In the town square.

Vultures circled overhead.

Earlier that morning where willows met road, a hare ventured out of the wild and into the square. A thunk under the vehicle made little impression on the car's driver but the scavengers were delighted.

They finalized the rabbit's transition back into the wild by roosting high in the eucalyptus branches where acidic excrement dripped to earth.

It fell on John.

Later, John's shoulder began to itch. His fingers found small knobby sprouts. Throughout the morning he worked his scaly skin loose. Finally, as the sun blazed overhead, two dark wings unfolded;

unconfined.

Bone and keratin solid around Jack's mouth slid along the handle. He pushed and thrashed until the door sprung. Flapping with a whoosh, the large, dark bird emerged. It caught an air thermal and rose without effort. Soon the vulture circled, awaiting another victim of the square.

Johnathan's replacement swept the office floor then sat at the square desk.

L. R. Conti is a science editor based in California. She worked as a bench scientist for many years until she began editing academic manuscripts professionally. Her stories often feature California State Parks where she spends much time watching vultures or inspecting slime molds. lisarconti.com

One Fine Day
by Chevanne Scordinsky

"Get thee behind me, Satan!"

"Alright now!"

"Have a good day, Miss Edith!"

"You too, baby."

Gwen waved at the neighbor. In a white polyester dress buttoned up to the neck and a lace fascinator flapping with her stride, she pounded the hot pavement. A leather-bound and worn Bible was tucked underneath her arm.

Gwen opened the front door and set the Bible on the kitchen table. She removed her white cotton gloves and placed them neatly at its side. She took off her dress and scanned it for stains. The summer had been dry and dusty.

She headed down to the basement where the fluorescent lights near the washer were much better. She peered through her bifocals at the hem, then up to the waist, carefully parting each pleat.

An acrid scent wafted into the air and Gwen scrunched her nose. Those damned sewer pipes.

A tall, hoofed beast with skeletal wings

materialized from a dark corner. A low growl resonated from its throat as it slowly approached. A bushel of harvested potatoes wrinkled and rotted in its wake. It leaned over Gwen, grazing the back of her neck with long talons.

"Where were you?"

Gwen turned and stared menacingly at the beast in her basement.

"Recruiting."

Chevanne is a writer and healthcare leader whose catalog of creative work is just taking shape. She explores genres from horror to the surreal. She is the author The FLARE, a Substack newsletter launched in July 2021 which includes fiction, personal essays, and poetry. Chevanne hopes to release a science fiction serial this year.

Hungry

by Sarah Jane Huntington

It was hard work running a pawnshop. Times changed and it got harder to con folks. Customers knew the value of the stuff they wanted to sell.

Take the woman, for example, she knew. Wretched fool.

The shop was quiet that day. I bought a stolen TV off some lowlife wanting drug money. I could sell it for triple the amount I paid and I put it in the window.

That's when I saw her. She was standing outside holding the hand of a boy of around nine or ten. I knew the type. No husband, no money, and likely stealing to make ends meet.

She came inside alone.

"My gold necklace," she said. "It's worth one hundred pounds."

"It's fake. I'll give you ten."

"Please, it's my son, he's hungry."

Lair.

"Ain't my fault," I told her. "Ten or nothing."

Tears sprang up in her sad eyes. I had no

sympathy. Scamming was my business.

Off she went, towing that skinny boy behind her.

Come closing time, I heard a low growl in the dark behind me.

A loose dog? No. That boy.

There he stood, changed.

He had razor-sharp teeth, a savage jaw, and vicious claws. It was true, he was very hungry indeed.

Sarah Jane Huntington is the author of 3 short story collections and 1 horror novel. She has been in several anthologies and has more due out this year.

Perception is in the Eye

by Rob Smales

The crow pecked the eye.

The surface, spongier than expected, gave beneath the striking bill, protecting its precious cargo a moment longer. The scavenger blinked, ruffling oil-slick feathers and shuffling black-clawed feet, bracing for a better strike. The owner of the eye, beyond all defense, merely stared blindly; the bird poised itself to thrust with exquisite care, a wicked gleam shining in its own ink-stain eyes.

The beak plunged, needle tip piercing the surface with a soft pop, splitting threads of tissue like a knife dropped in water. Again the beak came down, and again, a woodsman widening his cut, until the fibrous mass beneath the ocular bullseye lay revealed. The bill-tip gripped a thick strand and twisted. Lost its hold. Gripped again. A moist decomposition stink rolled out; the crow took no notice, merely tugged the morsel harder, harder—and with a jerk, the strand came free.

Then the crow was winging skyward, prize

gripped at the center of its length, raw ends fluttering, the bird's wild, glittering orbs fixed upon the distant site of its soon-to-be nest.

The scarecrow stood in the sun-drenched cornfield, cruciform and irrelevant, loose straw dribbling from its burlap head and painted eye, as another nesting crow lighted upon its shoulder.

Rob Smales's short stories have been published in over two dozen anthologies and magazines. His story "Photo Finish" was nominated for a Pushcart Prize and won the Preditors & Editors' Readers Choice Award for Best Horror Short Story of 2012. His story "A Night at the Show" received an honorable mention on Ellen Datlow's list of the Best Horror of 2014, and was also nominated as best short story by the Festival of Words. Most recently, his short story, "Wood You Love," was published in Wicked Creatures: A Journal of The New England Horror Writers, in October of 2021.

The Necromancer
by Emma Johnson-Rivard

"It shines," Anna said, tapping her fingers against the window. "It's beautiful."

There was a dead cat on the porch, all curled up in a ball. Frost on its fur, the mouth slightly parted. I didn't think that was beautiful, but Anna swung that way. Couldn't be helped. I called myself a poet, but Anna had turned out a little stranger.

"Bad luck," I said. "But it happens. It's just that time of the year. In fact—"

"Don't." Her eyes went sharp. "Don't ever fucking say that if you want to stay my sister."

Loneliness had a weight. She carried it in her hands. The way she drew nonsense lines against the window, driving through the delicate coating of frost. I'd always been the one to tell her no. I'd always been the one who knew she'd been lonely, and wanting. Always wanting. That she'd been wired lonely because of how we took all the strange. How we shunted it aside, closed those doors. And if I held to form, I'd be the one to call her back now.

Anna stared at me. And I stared back.

"I've got a name," she said. "A beautiful name."

I didn't stop her as she opened the door.

Emma Johnson-Rivard received her masters in creative writing at Hamline University. Her work has appeared in Tales to Terrify, Coffin Bell, and others. She currently serves as an editor at The Common Tongue, a dark fantasy magazine.

O Happy Dagger
by April Yates

Violet watched from the wings as Natalie, dagger in hand declared,

This is thy sheath;

there rust, and let me die.

She always stabbed down hard with the prop dagger, leaving a bruise upon her breast. Under silk sheets Violet would bestow feather light kisses on the tender flesh while muttering how silly Natalie was to suffer for her art.

"How else will it look real?"

So, night after night, Natalie died upon the stage.

Violet had been the props master for the theatre company for two years, enthralled by Natalie for three. She'd applied for the job to get closer to her, not content any longer to watch from the stalls. Violet had barely believed it when Natalie had spoken to her, asking if she'd like to get a drink sometime, had felt as if she must've died and ascended to heaven when she'd pulled her down for a kiss and asked if she'd like to come home with her.

It'd all been going so well until they'd recast Mercutio midway through the season with a woman whose beauty was second only to Natalie's.

Violet pressed the dagger into her thigh, the blade retracting harmlessly.

This will be your most realistic performance yet, my darling.

April Yates lives in Derbyshire England with her wife and two fluffy demons who masquerade as dogs. She should be writing, but is easily distracted by the squirrels in her garden and thoughts of lesbian vampires. Her debut novella, ASHTHORNE, a queer, historical horror-romance will be published by Ghost Orchid Press, Summer 2022. Her short stories appear in anthologies by Ghost Orchid Press, Black Hare Press, and Brigids Gate Press. She also suffers from a micro-fiction addiction and leaves them scattered across the web and in various anthologies.

*Twitter: @April_Yates_*

aprilyates.com

A Comforting Touch

by Wofford Lee Jones

Macy shuttered awake and out of the horrific nightmare in which she was dying. She immediately relaxed as she felt her husband's hand already gently rubbing her forehead. It was something he always did to calm her sleep-troubled spirit.

Macy sighed with relief and relaxed back into the comfort of her bed.

A dream, thank God! It was only a nightmare. Thank Jesus I don't have those too often.

She gave a slight smile to the comfort of Jake's soothing touch. The pressure tightened just a little more.

Macy was just drifting back into dreamland when her husband, Todd, turned over in the bed and draped one arm over her waist; the other became wedged between their bodies.

One hand draped over me. The other? Small of my back. The third?

A weird feeling of alarm crept over her. She put

two and two together. Her body was suddenly paralyzed by fear.

What the fuck is on my head?

Whatever thing that was on her head seemed to sense her alarm and clamped down harder and harder.

Instantly awake, she only had time to jerk her head toward Jake before a wet, black, gelatinous material slid down over her face silencing her screams.

Then, the real tightness began.

Wofford Lee Jones is the author of the Halloween-based horror novel 'Hell Night in Hopewell', a collection of dark stories,' Off the Beaten Path', and the supernatural thriller, 'Soul Dreams'. He works at Yates Engineering as a designer by day, by night, and on the weekends, he writes every chance he gets. In addition to writing, he enjoys art, photography, watching theater and movies, traveling, reading, drinking coffee, supporting his indie author friends, and unnerving his readers with his dark, delicious, and disturbing tales. He lives in Greenville, South Carolina, with his wife Laurie, and their four-legged son, Baxter.

Beauty is in the Eye of the Beholder

by Adele Evershed

Gertie looked at her newborn baby in horror. "He's deformed. What have I done, Ron? It was that smoked salmon at your Susan's birthday. I said it was off". Then, she started to wail, "It's all my fault."

Ron unwrapped his son and began to count his fingers and toes, but no matter how many times he did it, the number stayed the same. Ten perfect toes and ten perfect fingers. He shuddered and ran his fingerless hand over his head.

"Gert, wrap him up quick before your mother gets 'ere. We need time to decide what to do". This set Gertie wailing again, "I'm not putting him in an asylum. They work 'em in the factories when they're little, and when they can't work the machines anymore, they send 'em to the mines."

Ron patted his wife's stump and said, "Nobody's suggesting that. Bob knows a woman, she's not cheap, but she'll amputate a limb no questions asked. Rumor is she did the King's daughter. You'd never know to look at her that she was born ably bodied".

Ron looked speculatively at his son.

"If she charges the same for a limb as a hand, let's get his arm taken off. He'll be beautiful then."

Adele Evershed is an early years educator and writer. She was born in Wales and has lived in Hong Kong and Singapore before settling in Connecticut. Her prose and poetry has been published in several online journals including: Every Day Fiction, Ab Terra Flash Fiction Magazine, Grey Sparrow Journal, High Shelf, Tofu Ink Arts Press, Shot Glass Journal, Hole In The Head Review, and Monday Night Lit, to name a few. Adele has recently been shortlisted for the Pushcart Prize for poetry and the Staunch Prize for flash fiction (an international award for thrillers without violence to women).

thelithag.com

Bone for Bone

by Sue Marie St. Lee

Fred Johnson, funeral director at Johnson's Funeral Home whose motto is: 'Making Families Whole Again', headed to the old brick crematorium to collect Edna Thomason's ashes. Brushing them into the urn, he noticed her parietal bone remained intact—too large for the urn, no time left to cremate it.

With an ear-to-ear smile lighting up his face, Fred shouted, "What good fortune! This is exactly what Corporal Hentz needs!"

"Did you call me?"

A disembodied voice breathed upon Fred's shoulders.

Turning, Fred saw Corporal Hentz whose skull had been blown apart—lost to the dusts of World War II and buried without it. "Look, Hentz! This piece will make you whole again!" Fred held up the bone.

"No more headaches to be had!" Hentz's icy-blue breath encircled Fred's upper torso.

That night, Fred dug down and placed the bone in Hentz's grave alongside twenty-seven other skull bones he'd retrieved over the years in a similar fashion. He whispered, "Remember, Johnson's

Funeral Home makes families whole again."

Rising from the graveside, Fred collapsed. Knife-like pain in his skull overcame him. Looking up, he saw Edna, with twenty-seven ghosts, all puncturing and digging at his skull. They screamed, "Bone for bone! Your bones shall make us whole again!"

Chicago-born Sue Marie St. Lee lives in Oklahoma with her husband and Manx cat. A storyteller with a wild imagination since learning to talk, Sue's imagination persevered despite reprimands from her mother. Her stories have been published in domestic and international anthologies. Although her favourite writing genre is horror, she has written young adult speculative fiction with great success.

suemariestlee.home.blog/

Upon a Crooked Cross

by Keith Anthony Baird

Aiden toils in the attic room. Darius does not. This isn't how the boys normally spend their summer break. There is near-endless hammering. The elder of the two has been engrossed in his work for most of the afternoon. On arrival at the new family home, a storage box in the same space had yielded an interesting videotape for him to watch. It had given him… ideas. Three weeks later, his project is being realised. Muffled sounds punctuate the metallic chimes which drift down the sweeping staircase, to a hall with open door allowing the noise to entwine with the audio of an unwatched television.

Mom and Dad, back from the trip into town, unload the car and bring supplies inside. A shout for the boys is met with no response. Several tries and searching proves fruitless. They can only conclude the pair are off exploring the surrounding woodland. Later, much later, when they've not shown for dinner, does the thorough hunt begin. Father outside, mother within, their efforts are frantic. Inside, the space she's not yet tried beckons. The drop-down ladder creaks with each footfall and Mom gets a result in the search for her offspring:

Darius crucified on twisted timber.

Aiden beaming with pride.

Keith Anthony Baird is the author of The Jesus Man: A Post-Apocalyptic Tale of Horror, Nexilexicon, And a Dark Horse Dreamt of Nightmares, This Will Break Every Bone in Your Heart, Snake Charmer Blues, and A Seed in a Soil of Sorrow (Amazon and Audible). His novella, In the Grimdark Strands of the Spinneret, is out Nov 2022 (Brigids Gate Press). He's currently querying his novella, SIN:THETICA.

When not writing, you might find him up a mountain, snorkelling on a coral reef with his partner Ann, or having adventures with his grandson. Failing that, it's a good bet he'll be on Twitter.

Lending a Hand
by Adam Down

Three cracks mar the ward ceiling. Mark has come to know them intimately over the last few months.

"Tell me what you feel," Dr Linehan says from behind the white curtain that hides Mark's body from view.

He feels nothing. Since the accident it's always nothing. Linehan's experimental treatments haven't worked.

No . . . wait. A faint tingle from beyond the curtain, a long dormant nerve ending fires.

"Wow. I felt something. My hand."

"Yes, your thumb just twitched," Dr Linehan laughs, delighted, "Now concentrate. See what else you can do."

It's miraculous how quickly sensation returns. Only his hands, but he'll take anything after months of nothing. Mark can feel them both now, gives them an experimental stretch.

Two wet snaps issue from behind the curtain.

"What was that? Doctor?"

"Don't worry, it's perfectly normal. Just stay

calm, maintain control."

But it's too late. Mark's left hand spiders across the bed linen and tumbles to the floor. His right springs onto the bedside table and climbs the wall, nails digging into the wallpaper. The embossed roses are rough beneath his fingertips.

His hand leaps from the wall onto the white curtain and drags it off the rail.

Mark screams. His withered arms end in two bloody stumps.

Adam writes dark stories, and occasionally finishes them. His poison has leaked into the world in Ghost Orchid Press, Coffin Bell Journal, and Hellhound Magazine, amongst others. He can be followed and - at your own risk - interacted with on Twitter @AdamDownFiction

Acquitted on a Technicality

by Christopher Wood

Max listened to his dad's muffled snores creep in through paper-thin walls, could see in his mind's eye the old man's face half-buried in the pillow, the blanket nestled against his nose. It was a comfort to hear him sleeping again after everything that had happened. He suspected his dad cried alone, just as he did. A feeling, not quite pity, not quite regret, pricked his heart.

In the darkness, the squeak and creak of his bed ready to betray him, Max explored a body in transition. The bloom of youth wrought changes that he felt unable to articulate to the man in the next room. Changes to remain unspoken.

His hands traversed the shallow textures of his chest and stomach, muscles forming where once there was only puppy fat. He smiled, a tear forming, the phrase warmly reminding him of his mum. His hands continued to roam, stopping at the ragged line of inflamed tissue scarring his side: a 12-inch souvenir from the crash.

It itched. And then opened. A pleasant sensation, not dissimilar to taking a shit. Max ran his fingers over the double row of needle-sharp teeth lining the opening.

Hungry again. Ravenous.

Max recalled the drunk driver's address from the court case.

Christopher Wood resides in the historic city of Nottingham, Robin Hood country, with his wife, daughter, and roguish rescue cat. He is a Building Surveyor when he's not putting pen to paper but has lived many lives, particularly in heritage restoration, as a bricklayer, cinema usher and file store clerk. He has been published by Ghost Orchid Press and Crow's Feet Journal among other publications. He is currently working on a collection of short stories, as well as his debut novel.

Why Do Ghosts Open Cupboards?

by Ashley Lister

The question popped into my head as I entered the kitchen. Not for the first time I saw a cupboard door inexplicably open. Not for the first time I found myself staring at the contents: Mother's tin of soup. And not for the first time I wondered if there was a spirit in the house trying to convey a subtle message.

But what message was there in a tin of tomato soup, like the one I was now getting for my mother? Or yesterday? What message had there been in one of Mother's pre-packed Greek salads from Sainsbury's? Or the day before, when the cupboard door had opened to show a tin of Mother's favourite tuna?

If there was a ghost, a ghost trying to communicate with me, it was being remarkably obscure. Or I was being remarkably dense. Or maybe it was just being helpful?

I reached into the cupboard to retrieve the tin of soup, and my knuckles casually grazed the box of rat poison that sat next to the tin of soup. That box had also been beside the Greek salad, yesterday. And the tin of tuna the day before.

And as I prepared her lunch, I wondered, "Why do ghosts open cupboards?"

Ashley Lister is a prolific author of genre fiction, having written more than fifty full length titles, over a hundred short stories, as well as articles, academic papers and poems.

He is the author of How to Write Short Stories and Get Them Published, a five star writing guide that has been described as "A must have for anyone serious about publishing their short stories" and "Wish it had been available years ago."

His most recent title is Conversations with Dead Serial Killers, a horror story that incorporates aspects of the true crime genre.

The Other Inside Me

by C. R. Langille

When I look in the mirror, I see myself most of the time, and there is nothing to worry about. However, there are times I see someone else. They have my eyes. My facial structure. They even move when I do. But I know what I'm looking at isn't me.

I know it can't be me because when I see the other's image reflected in the mirror, I hate how their body looks. I hate their beard and how they dress!

Then, there are days when I look in the mirror and see the same image as before, but now it feels right. It's those days that I begin to question my sanity. Was what I felt before true, or was it just a strange phase?

But I know the truth. There's somebody else inside me, fighting to get out and getting stronger every day.

There are times when I can feel them, but I go about my day anyway. When I try and suppress the other, they remind me of my foolishness. They call me an imposter.

It was silly to think I could find victory by fighting

myself. The only way forward is to embrace the other inside me.

Besides… we are stronger together.

C.R. Langille spent many a Saturday afternoon watching monster movies with their mother. It wasn't long before they started crafting nightmares to share with their readers. They are a retired, disabled veteran with a deep love for weird and creepy tales. This prompted them to form Timber Ghost Press in January of 2021. They are an affiliate member of the Horror Writer's Association, a member of the League of Utah Writers, and they received their MFA: Writing Popular Fiction from Seton Hill University.

Rude Awakening

by Kevin Brooke

I wake to the shock of pain. My eyes heavy with crusted blood, I glance at the crumpled man beside me. His vacant expression is that of a dead man. There'd been a fight. Savage, brief. My recollection is hazy.

A woman is slumped on the sofa. Blood splatters the wall, the brutal effect of a bullet has smashed her face. She's holding a swaddle of blankets.

I remember her final words. 'Don't kill my boy', but the baby in her arms is motionless.

I open the barrel of my gun. One bullet left. The sound of sirens and the flash of blue light is followed by a shout.

'Armed police.'

My head throbs as I open the piece of paper in my hand. A contract. The image on the contract matches the dead man. The man I'd been sent to kill. My memory returns in a flood and none of it is good.

A sudden pain is acute. The knife in my side confirms a mortal wound and I glance at the woman. The baby in her lap stirs, the sound of his gentle whimper softens my sense of guilt. I place the gun inside my mouth, rest my finger on the trigger.

And squeeze.

Kevin Brooke tends to write short stories for adults and longer stories for young people. He has recently achieved several publications with Glittery Literary. Three of his longer stories have been published by Black Press, the most recent being a dystopian Young Adult story entitled 'The Objectors'. Occasionally, he dresses up as a Knight and tells stories as part of a storytelling partnership known as The Story Knights.

A Thought from the Damned

by Oli Jacobs

Everything is broken.

My arms? Smashed. My legs? Destroyed.

My back and neck? Snapped, crunched, and obliterated.

And all because my experiments were deemed "blasphemous".

Honestly…

These peasants wouldn't know what blasphemy is. To them, it is a word taught to them by manic zealots.

People who view science as a tapestry of terror. I've cured their diseases. I've healed their lame. I've even brought them fertility from barren wombs.

But when I bring about a discovery that will change the world, what happens?

I am hauled before their so-called authority. I am declared guilty of moral crimes. I am set upon by thugs and curs, armed with clubs and batons.

Beaten. Battered. Broken.

I am decried as an abomination. I am hailed as a monster. My acts seen as a violation against God.

Fools…

I am God.

Ha.

They'll find out soon enough.

I'm a patient man, you see. Very patient.

Even as I lie here with dirt filling my lungs, I can wait. I can wait a long time.

For my bones to set. For the strength to dig myself out of this shallow grave. For the moment to show them, all of them, what being immortal means.

Immoral?

Ha.

I'm beyond morality now.

Oli Jacobs is an independent author who has been telling his stories for nearly 10 years. He is best known for his epistolary novel Wilthaven, which came 9th in the Book Bloggers Novel of the Year Award 2021, and the Filmic Cuts series of short stories. He is also known to dabble in comedy (Kirk Sandblaster) and thrillers (Mr Blank). As always, he hopes you enjoy.

Sprouts

by Andy Spearman

Knock knock," goes the knock at the front door, and it isn't the jolly knock of a neighbour returning the Tupperware.

Neither is it the comforting knock of your parents coming home early from the theatre. Besides, this is their house – why would they knock?

"Knock knock." It's the kind of knock you hear and immediately wish you hadn't.

You realise that it's not a normal knock. It's more like a very loud, thoroughly displeased voice saying the actual words knock knock.

As you haven't answered yet, it gets a bit shirty: "Knock knock! Knockity knock knock!"

You really ought to go upstairs and hide in a closet.

You tiptoe to the door. You turn the doorknob. It doesn't open. Somehow it's locked from outside. The Knock – now with a capital K – won't let you open the door.

You spin around. Iron bars crash down, blocking your escape. Blinds slice over windows like a guillotine. The stairway vanishes. Lightbulbs explode.

You're trapped in total darkness. Your heart pounds through your chest.

There is a moment of unearthly silence …

… and then …

"Hey you!" The Knock's deep, watery voice fills the air, coming from every direction at once. "Aren't you the kid who didn't eat all their vegetables?"

Andy Spearman writes for children, mostly. Recent stories appear in Glittery Literary, The Caterpillar, and Parakeet Magazine. His middle-grade chapter book Barry, Boyhound was published by Knopf.

Spooky Stephanie

by Simon Paul Wilson

Nikki stares deeply into the mirror, a blackened candle clutched in her trembling hands. The girls reflection leers back at her, warped and twisted by the flickering flame she holds.

After taking her umpteenth deep breath, she finally manages to force out the words she's been too terrified to say.

"Spooky Stephanie, are you there?"

The five words shatter the silence of the room she's standing in. She waits a few moments before blowing out the candle and repeats the question.

"Spooky Stephanie, are you there?"

Several minutes pass. Nikki stands petrified in the dark, too scared to even breathe. It's only when her lunges start to scream for air that she relents. As she loudly inhales, she reaches over to her right and fumbles for the light switch.

"Mind your eyes, Bex."

Her fingers locate the switch and she flicks it on, narrowing her eyes as her bedroom is filled with light.

Nikki walks over to her dressing table with slumped shoulders. She tosses the extinguished candle aside.

"I don't get it," she says. "I thought we'd done everything the video said."

She turns to her friend Bex and pouts.

Bex stabs her in the face with a pair of scissors.

"I'm here," she says.

Simon Paul Wilson is the author of GhostCityGirl, See You When The World Ends, and Baggage, with Matt Wildasin. He lives in the U.K. with his wife and son. When not writing, Simon listens to post and prog rock at a very loud volume. He also plays a mean air-bass.

Follow him on Twitter @spwzen

A Body to End all Agonies
by A.R. Martinez

The moon changed Naura. Beneath gentle white light her boundaries decomposed. Dilated pores vomited her sloppy self onto the ground. The sleeve of her used up skin collapsed in folds of cytolytic cells. Primordial slime pulsated with a rumble of blood-black bubbles. A dominant pustule ballooned, forming her obsidian egg, a dark twin to the celestial ovary floating above, its partner hidden, conjoined light nurturing a child that would be hungry once hatched.

Naura had resisted the first change, had denied the primal destiny she'd risen to fulfill. Acceptance invaded her cells and pulped her brain. Welcoming her fate became easy as a fantastic mistake.

Oils she oozed sank into a screaming Earth. Naura infected the soil, what grew there, and what ate that. And what ate that. Festering within the swelling egg spread. Fleshly organisms malfunctioned. They howled a chorus heralding her immanence. They begged for her execution capable mouth and molten womb. She was a remaking machine. Blessings she belched scoured the planet, cleansed the world.

Cracks split the nacreous egg. Pus extruded from the wound. Black veins webbed from the fissure, reached for the stars it extinguished. The Pergatum Tree rose from Naura's ruined body and began the dread work of unnamable angels.

A.R. Martinez grew up in New Orleans and now lives in Jefferson Parish as beggars can't be choosers. In a hurricane-proof townhouse, she lives with two cats and fosters a third with special needs. She writes mostly dark fantasy, science fiction, and horror. Depending on your viewpoint she is a lifelong experiencer or manages alien abduction syndrome. Take your pick as she has no idea what's going on. You can find her on Twitter at @ARoseMartinez.

Landmark

by John Marentay

That house had stood there for as long as anyone in town could remember. It was a landmark. I couldn't let them demolish it. So I snuck in, past the bulldozers and the security guard, to hang a simple sign from that turret. It just read "SHAME" and was written in big red letters on a white sheet.

It seemed older inside than I thought it would be, the floors all spongy and soft. Everything was dirty and smelled of mildew. I started up the steps to the central tower. If I hung the sign from there, everyone in town would see it.

I was the hero, and the house was happy to see me.

It was the third set of stairs that collapsed underneath me. Falling, I tumbled back to the main landing. The ceiling followed, crushing me.

Awakening just as the sun rose, I couldn't feel my legs. My arms were pinned to my side. I tried to yell, but I couldn't get my breath. Pushing down the panic, I tried to inch out, rolling back and forth to get space. It hurt, but there was progress. I was going to make it. I was going to live.

Then I heard the bulldozers start.

John is just an average guy. He loves telling stories, taking inspiration anywhere he can get it. His concentration is mainly on microfiction, finding it immensely satisfying to build a visceral world in as few words as possible. He currently resides in almost rural Florida.

Providence

by Cassondra Windwalker

Hunger is a hollow bone that looks like a desert stone, clenched in the teeth of a dog whose tongue is too dry to slaver. It lies in the sun and casts no shadow, it gleams undaunted on even a moonless night.

The man played hunger against his thigh like a castanet as he walked, his every thought set to its rhythm. He prowled the trash heaps scattered along the roadsides, but everyone else was hungry, too. Food wrappers were licked clean, aluminum cans shone like silver. His belly quivered, flaccid beneath a rope belt, and his knees shook as he trudged on through pelting heat.

He did find meat eventually. It took a while, in the harsh sunlight, for his eyes to adjust and his brain to register the sight. Children scoured the trash heaps, too, hunting for plastic bottles to sell to restaurants to fill with water for their patrons. They were like wild goats, he realized. Provender from the Creator, to sustain the beloved. Wary and nimble like goats, still they were not so surefooted, not so feral as he, and their meat was sweeter and more tender than any game.

Hunger is a hollow bone, clenched in the teeth of

a dog.

Cassondra vacillates between hermit and troubadour while doing most of her writing from the southern coast of Alaska. This particular story, though, was composed while on the northern coast of Madagascar. Her novels and full-length poetry collections are available in bookstores and online. Her romantic horror, Hold My Place, was published by Black Spot Books in January 2022.

Don't Think

by Adam Hulse

"Don't think about it, just do it." That's what they keep saying to me.

Whenever I feel sad or angry, they call to me, sing their songs, and make me feel like anything is possible. While I'm waiting here, I'll give you an example of what living with them has been like for me. I had a girl and for a little while I had a reason, a purpose to behave. Then she left me, and I was lost. Not for long though, because they called to me again.

"Meet us at the train station," they sang.

So I stopped crying and moping around my place. For a little while it was our place but now it's just my place again. They told me that's how things go sometimes. They told me which train to get on and which stop to get off. Then as I walked around aimlessly, they decided which house I should sneak into because the back window was open.

"Get upstairs," they told me.

So I did as they asked, and I lay patiently under your bed waiting for you to return home. I hum the beautiful songs they sing to me. You won't believe the songs I can sing for you.

It took a global pandemic for Adam to once more create his own dark worlds to escape into. Adam's debut, the Tales of Tupuqa three novella series was published by Raven Tale Publishing in 2021. His poem The Summit made Punk Noir Magazines "21 Essential Punk Noir Stories and Poems" list. Adam is raising two strong daughters in a small town in decline within the North-West of England.

Twitter: @HulseAdam

To Crave the Light

by Mia Lofthouse

I run my hands over the thing. The darkness that is my world is as pressing as ever. His shirt beneath my fingers moves like water. I have made him delicate.

I find his neck and press into the flesh as if I am expecting him to return from his own darkness. The darkness I have put him in. There is no pulse.

My father is dead. I can feel the smile stretch across my face.

You'll never leave me, little duck, he had said. *I will not allow it.* And then pain, searing, terrible. Blackness burst into life as he held my head. The burning liquid fell across my face, taking the congealed matter that had been my eyes, with it.

I touch his forehead now, run my fingers through his hair. I lie on my stomach, move my lips close to his ear. "Stay still little duck," I say.

I reach to my side, grasp the handle, the metal is cool. I search his face, find the delicate skin of his lids and prise them open.

His eyes come out with a wet popping sound.

I hold them in my hands, lie on my back, then drop them into the hollows above my nose.

Mia is a twenty-one year old, UK based writer. She is currently taking a Masters degree in Creative Writing and writes both short stories and novels. In 2017 she was a finalist in the Wicked Young Writer Award and more recently, her short story, The Road Home, has been published in Personal Bests Journal, Issue 3.

The Changeling
by Maureen O'Leary

The boy emerged from the fountain with blue lips. He wrapped himself in a discarded canvas tarp and peeked at me from the tattered edge. When night fell he remained out there and so I knew what he was.

I gazed through the leaded window of my apartment, a hot cup of chai steaming the glass. I thought of iron, or silver, or mugwort, some protection. I thought of a saucer of milk, of dandelion, or bluebell, some gift.

Lest you think I am paranoid about faeries let me ask you: How did I know not to look him in the eye? How did I know not to risk the milk or bread, or flower? I displeased one when I was a child and so they took my brother and left behind a troll. Lest you think I am paranoid again let me ask you: What other reason could there be for the monster of my brother? His rolling gut, his cold eyes, the way he is now fifty and sleeps on mom's couch and refuses to get a job?

I slept and in the cold morning frost found the tarp remained with a boy shape within but no longer peering at anyone anymore.

Maureen O'Leary lives in Sacramento, California. Her work appears in Coffin Bell Journal, The Horror Zine, Ariadne Magazine, and Bandit Fiction. She is a graduate of Ashland MFA.

Scatter Me
by Kathryn Tennison

Cece knew she shouldn't drink from the river. It probably contained a thousand deadly parasites. But she'd been hiking for over an hour, and she'd only now realized she left her water bottle in the car.

"Just a mouthful," she said, crouching beside the tantalizing water.

She scooped it up in her palm and brought it hastily to her dry lips. Then again and again. The fourth drink tasted a little strange, and when she looked down at her hand she saw that it was flecked with something black.

"Ick!" she said, wiping it on her shorts.

The river, which had appeared clear before, was now full of something dark and flaky. As quickly as it had appeared, it was gone, rushing downstream. She was still wondering what it was when voices drifted toward her out of the trees.

"It's what she wanted."

"I know, but it feels weird."

"This was one of her favorite spots."

Two figures appeared, one holding a silver urn

that reflected the bright sunlight. When they saw Cece, they froze. Their eyes met hers. She looked at her hands, which were streaked with ashy remains. Then she hunched over, heaving, and black goop dribbled from her mouth onto the rocky ground.

Kathryn Tennison received her MFA in creative writing from Butler University in Indianapolis. She currently lives in Arkansas with her husband, two cats, and one enormous dog. When she's not writing, she enjoys gardening, baking vegan goodies, and watching horror movies.

That Bony Light
by A C Clarke

He crouches over his workbench, unravelling the
twisted threads that tied a life together. Here a robin
fallen from its perch semaphores surrender, legs
pointing to the ceiling. There a fox, white bib smeared
dirty red, stares from unwinking eyes. He'll resurrect
them into poses whose liveliness drives home how
dead they are.

Will you walk into my parlour?

She steps into his cabinet of curiosities, shopsoiled
river-nymph, hair escaping from its snood and tangled
as waterweed, dress grey with the dust of a London
summer. She moves from sun to darkness, her eyes
taking time to register the duelling frogs, the bottled
baby, the Frenchman leering from the corner, too
many teeth in his skull.

I take pride in my skill with knife and needle.

She breathes fetid incense of dusty feathers,
feathery skin. She tastes it in the tea he brews from

leaves like mouse-droppings. It's on the hand which passes her the cup, the fingers which briefly nudge hers when she takes it.

Let me lift your hair into safe-keeping,

She watches his deliberate movements, sees how his busy hands could burrow her, search her out from femur to stapes. He'd know her as no-one has before. His fingers play with a scalpel

A C Clarke, a poet living in Glasgow, has published five full collections and six pamphlets, two of the latter in collaboration with Maggie Rabatski and Sheila Templeton. Her fifth full collection, A Troubling Woman, came out in 2017. She was one of four winners in the Cinnamon Press 2017 pamphlet competition with War Baby. She has been working on poems about Paul and Gala Éluard, and their Surrealist circle. The first set of these was published as a pamphlet, Wedding Grief by Tapsalteerie in 2021.

The Brass Mirror

by Brian Barnett

The two men stared at the brass surface before them. The robbery was a bust. There was no money in the cash drawer and after the alarm, they only managed to grab this useless chunk of metal.

"Shop of oddities, indeed," Carrigan scoffed.

"Well it looks nice, anyway. I can almost make out my reflection." Morris watched as his face distorted and stretched around the reflective surface.

Carrigan nervously glanced out the window for the fifth time as he typically did after breaking the law.

Morris used his sleeve to polish the brass. Maybe it'll be worth something after all. As he did, it seemed to resonate a low hum. It was just loud enough to hear, but it was there.

He rubbed the mirrored surface more vigorously. A constant hum filled the room. As he did, his vision blurred a bit. It was almost like he was watching one of those fancy 3D films without the glasses.

But there was something else in his vision. A

hooded creature with tentacle arms. It turned towards him.

He quickly stopped polishing the surface and shoved it across the table.

"Well, is it worth anything, Morris?"

Morris, sick to his stomach, answered. "No, not worth anything at all."

Brian Barnett is the author of the middle grade novellas Graveyard Scavenger Hunt and Chaos at the Carnival. He has over three hundred publishing credits in dozens of magazines and anthologies such as the Lovecraft eZine, Spaceports & Spidersilk, Blood Bound Books, and Scifaikuest.

Cursed Words

by Steve Bridger

I am not afraid of tarantulas—the bigger and hairier, the better. Spiders could climb my bedroom walls, and I would sleep like a log.

Some people faint at the slightest drop of blood, even wincing at gore on television.

I, for one, like murder. Sinking my teeth into virgin flesh in the dead of night doesn't faze me.

Blood, bile and violence, bring it on.

I am stronger than most.

The perils of sunlight don't scare me. Overly-seasoned garlic bread fails to fill me with dread or panic. I can wear sunblock. Avoid carbohydrates. I'm happy when demons crawl through cracks in my basement floor. Ghosts can wait like harbingers of death over my coffin. I find comfort. I know no fear.

Over flickering candlelight, past the plastic roses and leather wine menu, I watch my date's face in horror. Dianne's full red lips curl and open, speaking a chilling phrase.

Her words hang in the air like a curse. Unspeakable doom fills the restaurant with danger.

She mouths the words: "Long-term relationship."

I quickly withdraw from the table, my ice-cold hands sweating.

I cower, stinging from the acidic word, "Commitment."

I hastily excuse myself from the table, move to the bathroom, and never return.

Steve Bridger is a sleepy animator and illustrator originating from Essex in the UK. He's entered into several amateur writing competitions, coming second in a short story competition and shortlisted in another. While by day his main focus is design and illustration; by night, he enjoys creative writing and attempting flash fiction. He currently lives in Cheltenham with some house plants.

Parallel

by Susan Earlam

I wait there in the black. I can't tell if my eyes are open or closed and yet I know I'm not asleep. Soundless lights arrive over a new and distant horizon. They come towards me directly. I steady myself, some remembered instinct tries tempting me to move to a safer spot, but I stand my ground. I hold myself at the coordinates because they won't find me if I move. I'll be lost again, forever this time.

The lights come closer until they are all I can feel. I stay firm and brace myself. Beams sweep over me, I must be lit up. They must see me. But nothing. Perhaps I didn't register on their machines, maybe I don't exist anymore. They can't collect what isn't there. I make an attempt to call out. They stay for a moment more, did they hear me? I try making myself as big as I can, but they turn and leave. The shimmering trail of light disappears back over the horizon, which then fades quickly after them. My insides spin. I clutch at myself, but feel nothing. I remember my life before, the people I love must think I'm gone, but I'm still here, alone and questioning everything.

116

Since 2010, Susan has written for a variety of media outlets, but the call of the strange and unusual grew irresistible. Now she mixes words like potions at her laptop in Cheshire, England. She procrastinates by writing shorter, and weirder, stuff. Her first novel, eco-horror Earthly Bodies, is out now.

@susanearlam on Twitter and Instagram

Website https://susanearlam.com/

Scab

by Cynthia Gómez

Lucía had bills to pay. So she told herself she'd be forgiven for slipping past the picket line of her coworkers on strike, and she didn't give any more thought to what she had done, even the day she looked down at her hand and she saw it: a blotch, just above her wrist, scarlet and thick, on a hand she had no memory of having scraped. But there it was, the body's way of reacting to damage, of trying to heal. A scab.

Just as the picket lines swelled with each day, the scarlet patch spread further over her hand, edges puffy and red. She would look down at the box she was packing to find the bandage soaked through, the scab sloughing off, blood staining the cardboard, while around her the speed alarms screeched.

By Friday it had reached her knuckles, and she was written up for falling behind minimum speed.

That Sunday she logged into the scheduling app, hand wailing as it navigated the keypad. Blood dripped onto the phone, smearing the words that stayed the same even as she entered her password over and over, the login screen flashing the same red letters every time: sorry, that Team Member does not exist.

Cynthia Gómez is a writer and researcher living in Oakland. She writes horror and speculative fiction and has a particular love for themes of revenge, retribution, and resistance to oppression. She has stories in The Acentos Review, Strange Horizons, and the collection Antifa Splatterpunk. You can find her on Twitter at @cynthiasaysboo.

The Family Whistle

by Matthew Mitchell

"Sit here," Uncle said, "and listen."

"I don't want to." The boy shook his head.

"What did you say?" His voice rang out like a shot.

"Mind your Uncle," Papa called to the porch from the kitchen. "Don't make me come out there."

"See," Uncle said, "got yourself in trouble."

The boy stood. Tears welled in his eyes.

"Your kid ain't listening, Earl."

A clattering of dishes; Papa's footsteps.

"Uh-oh." Uncle smiled. The trenches of his teeth were grey. "You're in for it now…"

"Okay," the boy said, voice rising. "I'll listen!"

Papa's footfalls stopped short of the screen-door.

"That's better," Uncle said. He reached inside his checkered suit.

The boy sat. He heard Papa retreat to the sink.

Uncle produced a wooden reed, no wider than a blade of grass. He put the stick to his lips and blew; a sickly scream whistled out, impossibly loud. The boy winced.

Inside the house, Papa began to howl. Porcelain shattered against a wall. Papa's legs kicked at the floor, a full sprint for the porch. The boy began to cry.

"Now, now, nephew," Uncle stood and hopped off the deck. "No crying." He backed away.

"It won't hurt much," Uncle said, with both eyes on the door.

Matthew Mitchell is a horror fiction and comic book writer from the Ozarks. His comic books have appeared in Heavy Metal magazine and Image comics. Matthew's fiction has been published in "In the Shadow of the Horns: A Black Metal Horror Anthology" and "Feral: A Journal of Ozarkian Gothic." Matthew is the co-creator of the comic anthology "Horrorium."

Room 206

by Jack Harding

I live in a room. I live like dust in a room. Like a black, malignant cancer in the corner of one's brain. I do not move. I do not speak. I do not do much of anything except watch . . . and wait.

Thin, grey sunlight creeps through the gap in the old, stained curtains, and I look upon the empty bed and wonder how long it's been. A year? A decade? It's hard to tell. It's been a long time. A long, uneventful time without a soul to play with. Without a mind to haunt.

I am old. I am alone. I would tell you what I am, but I do not know.

A young woman—plump and fair, comes by now and then to clean the space but she never stays long enough for me to really find my groove. A pity. Maybe the owner of this grand old establishment has grown wise to my ways. So I wait. I wait.

And then . . . I wait some more—I hear footsteps.

Slow, approaching footsteps. I hear the twinkle of keys against the hollow timber of the old, chipped door. I hear voices. The door swings open, and two damned souls step inside room 206 of The Blackridge Hotel.

Jack was born and raised in Portsmouth, United Kingdom. He divides most of his spare time between running, reading, watching old movies, and doing absolutely nothing with his partner, Rachel. His favourite authors are Ray Bradbury, Richard Matheson, Alan Moore and Stephen King. His favourite books are The Illustrated Man, I Am Legend, From Hell, and The Dead Zone. Jack's debut short story collection, Ripper Country, is set for publication through Bloodrites Horror Publishing in January 2022. He also has numerous stories featured in horror anthologies across several publications.

Clever Cait Shee
by Syreeta Muir

Cait Shee was a bit of a klepto. Age ten she considered herself, somewhat romantically, a kind of Land Corsair, Maid Marian-type.

It started with cats. She had a natural affinity for them, her mum would tell people—probably because she knew Cait was listening—on account of her rare eye-condition: pupils vertically slit, leonine. Always knew the shiny ones would give her what she wanted without much fuss and she knew how to make things click.

Content at first, sipping on slippery, black cat souls, for the time she could keep them still: That was good, she'd think, good and fair—no laws violated, or vows broken. She was not some ordinary Sea Reaver. She understood the power of a fair exchange, just as her real parents had before her, the night they'd left her in the powder pink crib in place of the babe they spirited away.

But cats were never quite satisfying enough. As her palette matured she craved more subtle flavours. Human things. The variety was infinite, and when she grew bored she could just siphon them off in one big go. She smiled at them, like a grimalkin-eyed Pirate Jenny, blowing them little thank you kisses as their lights went out.

Syreeta Muir's got your nose. Boop. Writing in Versification, Daily Drunk Mag, The Disappointed Housewife, Sledgehammer Lit, A Thin Slice of Anxiety, and Misery Tourism. Photography in Barren Magazine and Olney Magazine.

Twitter: @hungryghostpoet

It's Time

by John Holmes

Father never allows me to cut with his scythe.

Despite the blisters on his weathered hands and his old, aching body, 'no' is always the answer.

Today, as he stops to rest his tired limbs, I ask him once more.

He runs his thumb over the sharp, shiny blade, strokes his grey beard and announces: 'Son, the time has come. '

He leans forward, hooks the scythe around my neck and pulls me towards his panting chest.

'Time,' he continues, 'cannot be stopped. There are no rules that allow for 'Dead Time'. My work has to last longer than any life time.'

My throat has started to leak bright droplets of blood onto the metal.

'In this world,' he says, seemingly unaware of my discomfort, 'time is not inherited from Father to Son.'

I give him my best, puzzled look. One that doesn't require too much head movement.

'It's Time.'

As he speaks these words, he expertly flicks his wrists.

Father Time holds his son's face close to his mouth, sucks in the boy's last shallow breath and then lowers him to the ground.

With youthful energy, he grabs his hour glass, turns it over, rests his scythe on his shoulder and strides away. Time moves on.

John Holmes, based in the North East of England, is a writer of short fiction. A previous winner of the The Times Short Crime Fiction Story prize and in the last 12 months has had work appear in Paragraph Planet, 101 Words, Fragmented Voices and Ellipsis Zine. He is the co-author of Rough Rides, a mountain biking guide book - and when he isn't writing, he's out on his bike exploring new routes.

Wolf Birds

by Hazel Ragaire

Comfortable in high perches, the ravens track and sentries shrill danger, warning their wolves. The intelligent birds protect forest creatures from harm, their hyperpalliums assessing and planning. Unaware, the hunters pursue.

Breaking camp, the hunters trek deeper ready to kill, shrill cries haunting their movements. Leading the wolves into position, the unkindness prepares. The first wave descends, surrounding their targets, gouging their faces. Screaming men run in different directions, arms flailing, throwing the birds off as they can. Black ribbons weave through the trees, driving their dinners further apart, towards the north, east, and west, towards the waiting wolves. Dropping their guns, the hunters resort to knives. Several ravens scream, sacrificing their bodies for sheaths defiantly plunging their beaks into soft necks or eyes, calling blood.

Snarling, the wolves seek arteries. Merciful hunters, they bleed those bent on harming the pack quickly. Raising bloodied throats skyward, they howl. The ravens join, croaking joy before helping the wolves rend the clothes. The ravens collect buttons and rings, hopping them safely to the side before returning to feast. Eating first, the wolves warm their bellies, retreating for the ravens to pick the bones clean.

Full, the ravens patrol their skies, ever-watchful, and the wolves drag the bodies away.

Only ideas outnumber the books in Hazel's home. Breathing life into monster monstrosities and the just plain weird with a dash of horror or a sprinkle of sci-fi is kinda what she does. Enjoy published works in several Ghost Orchid Press anthologies, Halloween Horror 3, Wimbledon Common, and 42 Stories as well as Fudoki and Microfiction Monday Magazine. Find her at www.hazelragaire.com or Twitter @HRagaire to enjoy what her brain dreamt up.

The Surprising Accuracy of Late Night TV

by Corey Farrenkopf

An ancient television sits in the basement of our ancestral home.

We're remodeling.

I plan to disconnect the antenna until the television flicks on late at night. The crackle of old speakers draws me down the basement steps, half-asleep, the playroom awash in gray light.

On the screen my grandfather lies in a hospital bed, IVs tracing veins. The sheets rise until a final breath heaves from his lungs.

The next night, the same tone drags me from dreams. On the screen a cousin runs through a cornfield. He trips, falling beneath the wheels of a tractor.

For a month, I witness family members meet their deaths.

Each night I promise myself I'll remove the TV, sever the antenna and the connection to that unknowable dark void, loop ended.

But I don't.

I watch my father die. A fishing accident, waders filling with brackish water.

The next night, my own face fills the screen. I'm in the woods behind the house. There's a snarl at my heels, a gasp in my throat.

I lean forward, finger depressing the power button.

As the screen fades to black, a chorus of wolves rises from the pines at the edge of our property.

The TV is never wrong.

Corey Farrenkopf lives on Cape Cod with his wife, Gabrielle, and works as a librarian. His short stories have been published in Tiny Nightmares, The Southwest Review, Cemetery Gates Media, Catapult, Flash Fiction Online, Reckoning, Bourbon Penn, and elsewhere. He is the Fiction Editor for The Cape Cod Poetry Review.

Twitter @CoreyFarrenkopf

CoreyFarrenkopf.com

The Sudden Discovery of Your Near Invincibility While Falling from an Exploded Plane
by Patrick Barb

Your hair's on fire as you plummet, ground rushing up to offer a lumpy permafrost conclusion to this unexpected descent. At this height, ice crystals form on eyelashes, the cracked flesh of lips, and inside nostrils, but melt just as fast. Your gulping breaths fill with the foul odor of charred flesh (your own and others) and the aforementioned roasting follicles.

Reduced to ashes, the others travel faster. They'll litter the ground, marking your impact site. Or the wind will grab them, sending them far away. Perhaps the pilot's ashes will settle on a beach, decorating seashells ebony and silver.

Sizzling hunks of the puddle-jumper plane you'd taken for this last delivery—"A simple job, bud," Boss says—form a blazing slurry around you, adding to the roar of blood pumping in your ears. You're numb enough for your inferno crown to register as less than a tickle. So you certainly can't be expected to notice when the fuselage hunks burrow under skin. You always wondered what it might be like to have a piercing. When you land, you'll be studded metallic.

You're falling. But you're not dead yet. So, you have more time to think about surviving.

You have more time to think about revenge.

Patrick Barb is an author of weird, dark, and horrifying tales, currently living (and trying not to freeze to death) in Saint Paul, Minnesota. His short fiction appears in Diabolical Plots (forthcoming), the Humans are the Problem anthology, and Boneyard Soup Magazine, among other publications. His debut novella Gargantuana's Ghost is coming from Grey Matter Press in August 2022. In addition, he is an Active member of the Horror Writers Association. For more of his work, visit patrickbarb.com.

Summoning the Gone

by Alexis DuBon

Light a candle, guide the dead. The flame will sing through darkness. One for money, two for health, three for love. Tremulous, each stands alone, you wonder where to place them. Light the wick, call a name— some who wander are lost.

Lead them through the gossamer, watch them file in.

Call a name, the name that's been suspended on your tongue. Now you can release it, as you watch the shadows pass. One is sure to be the right one, one is your familiar. Yet as they march with silent steps, none answer to the sound of your voice.

You try again, you shout it through cupped hands. Empty faces, slumped and vacant, each figure travels onward. Not one recognizes the name you are now screaming.

Masses are gathering quickly, where before there was a trickle. Endlessly seeping in, filling the room, choking the flames. But that's been the trick all along, you realize.

Three lit candles burn weaker apart—together, a nosegay of fire clutched tight in your fist, they blaze. Come back to me.

Finally, a face shines through, illuminated against the mural of strays. You know this face. The one you sought. But now the sun is rising and the room again is empty.

Alexis DuBon is a work of fiction. Any resemblance to actual persons, living or dead, is purely coincidental. You can find her in the Hundred Word Horror anthology series by Ghost Orchid Press, Field Notes From a Nightmare by Dread Stone Press, A Woman Built By Man by Cemetery Gates Media, A Quaint and Curious Volume of Gothic Tales by Brigids Gate Press, on the Horror Oasis YouTube channel, The Wicked Library podcast, and on twitter at @shakedubonbon.

Trials and Tibialations

by Sara Crocoll Smith

Care to follow me where the singing ends?

To where Earth's stomach churns, where our flesh makes friends?

Cling boldly and bodily as long as you dare. Yet it's best not to linger, to be caught unaware.

For as sure as you're alive, you'll suffer, you'll perish.

Break a few bones on the way toward that marriage.

For stars' dust you are and to stars' dust you'll return—miraculous, fluid.

No lead in the moment breaks you, mars you, decrees you ruined.

For what leaves you with scars is but a wisp of smoke's past.

None of what plagues you ever can last.

Come they do, go they must—careful wishing away what withers and rusts.

A dream within a dream it may be. Dream or nightmare, it's a smear in the rearview to eternity.

I see you, nestled in transient skin. Don't forget it wrinkles, it crumbles, it sins.

It also transforms, nourishes, blooms. Rejoice in your heart, make abundant room.

The singing may cease, but on lives the tune.

Where hallowed ground is found, anointed in cordial soil, we'll soon depart this mortal coil.

We'll become light and free, leaving behind only calcified density.

What's there to fear? Only the stray tibia, my dear.

Sara Crocoll Smith is the author of the ghostly gothic horror series Hopeful Horror. She's also the publisher and editor-in-chief of Love Letters to Poe, a haven to celebrate the works of Edgar Allan Poe and encourage the creation of gothic fiction tapped from the vein of Poe. For an exclusive morsel of ghosts and daylight horror, visit SaraCrocollSmith.com/Ivy to get the free short story "The Strangle of Ivy."

Delicacies

by Matthew McGuirk

In a way it makes me laugh, but not really. The way they watch over us without even being seen really makes me cringe. Waiting for us to hit that ripe age, the age where the digits have just the right taste to them and they've had us produce the offspring necessary for the food supply to continue to prosper. Sure, some protested and were slaughtered on the spot, blood spilling from the severed necks of their children first, then spouses and finally their life taken slowly, their bones being ground with a mortar and pestle that could turn cities to powder.

We watched the rite of passage, the person marching silently away, not sure when they'd be swept up and the parts of them deemed a delicacy sliced off and the rest of them discarded to rot as fertilizer for sides. Nobody knew why the digits were their favorite or why the remainder of the carcass was left–trimming the fat–but we went on living a life that lasted until it didn't and being purposeful to ourselves until we were deemed ready to whatever these things were and that's how life is and how it had been since before any of us could remember.

Matt McGuirk teaches and lives with his family in New Hampshire. BOTN 2021 nominee with words in various lit mags and a debut collection with Alien Buddha Press called Daydreams, Obsessions, Realities available on Amazon and linked on his website.

Website: http://linktr.ee/McGuirkMatthew Twitter: @McguirkMatthew Instagram: @mcguirk_matthew.

The Grey Lady
by Helen Mills

Lucy started working as many shifts as possible at the Castle Hotel to get away from him. It was "their little secret" he whispered to her one night, his sour breath warm in her ear.

The job was an escape.

The kitchen porter told her about the Grey Lady – a ghost who watches from a window in the North turret. The story goes that the Grey Lady waited month after month at that window for her husband to return from battle. When the news came that he had died she jumped out of the window as she could not live without him.

Lucy would make up any reason to spend time in the North turret where she felt the Grey Lady's presence. She too started to sit at the window. She too started to feel her sadness. Then, one morning, she saw him - walking up the drive, rage in his clenched knuckles. It had been found out.

In that moment she suddenly felt she understood. A kinship transcended the centuries between them. The Grey Lady did not jump because her husband had died in battle, she had jumped because he returned.

Lucy opened the latch, felt the cold air on her skin

and stepped out.

Helen Mills is a professional research manager who has recently turned her hand to writing fiction.

She is particularly interested in writing about the hidden female experience and things that go bump in the night.

She has left her busy city life behind to return to where she grew up in rural Northumberland with her young family.

They Came

by Steven Ross

The point of the scalpel shone like a beacon lighting the way to madness as it shook in his trembling hands. This was the way – his only way – forward. That's what they told him, at least.

They had come to him, always just at the edge of his vision, to guide his path home. He knew them well, despite their misshapen skulls and twisted, bloody bodies; they were his kin. The others, the ones that lived their dull, monochrome existence (if you could call it living) couldn't grasp – couldn't…feel…what he felt, what he knew: Another path, one of glorious technicolor splashes of crimson, existed. All that it took to enter this world was to pay the fee.

His initial attempts to pay the way were barely visible in the dimly lit room, but the humming of bloated flies, fat from their feast, was sufficient to identify them: bodies – parts really, sticky and glistening in their putrescence. Their stench hung oppressively in the air, but he no longer noticed. The payment wasn't accepted, he had to offer a more personal form of currency.

Breathing slowly, he calmed his trembling and plunged the blade into his eye socket, removing the orb with surgical precision.

Finally…they came.

Steven Ross is a Canadian Author and Poet hailing from just outside of the Nation's Capital. A weaver of dark words, with a penchant for penning tales both visceral and disturbing, you will often find him lurking in the bloodstained shadows of the horror genre.

Never one to be satisfied with being cast in a single mold though, he also enjoys writing poetry focused on all aspects of life: from pain, loss and suffering to tales of romance and erotic desire, to good ol' fashioned humor.

Tick. Tock.

by Joe Haward

He woke to the sound of ticking. His head burning with agony, he attempted to move, but found himself tied to a chair fastened to the floor, his wrists and ankles bound tightly. The room was poorly lit, revealing nothing but a dirty carpet and grey walls. On the table in front of him was a clock, the second hand slicing time away. Next to the clock was a digital timer, counting down. Bright red numbers displayed three hours, thirty one minutes. Suddenly it reset, showing seventy two hours. He screamed and called for an hour, but no-one came. Rocking his body back and forth, he tried to break free from his binds, but to no avail.

He fell asleep watching the timer, the numbers reading sixty three hours, twenty minutes as he closed his eyes.

Waking up, a few hours later, the timer reset again.

The sound of the ticking second hand ripped through his brain.

He tried to stay awake, but eventually lost the battle at fifty three hours and one minute.

Jolting himself awake, the timer reset.

The room stank from his own filth, the air claustrophobic.

He wondered what would happen if the timer finally reached zero? Did he want it to?

Rev Joe Haward is an author, poet, and heretic. His freelance journalism challenges political and religious corruption and hypocrisy. Writing horror, noir, and transgressive fiction and poetry, Joe's work has featured in various places. His debut poetry collection, Heresy (Uncle B. Publications) will drop in 2022. Find him at joehaward.co.uk or on Twitter @RevJoeHaward.

The Possessed

by Matthew Schultz

"Don't take any pictures!" Marie warned. "And don't touch anything."

Brian's thumb hovered just above the screen of his iPhone. "Why not?" he asked.

"This place gives me the creeps. I don't want you bringing any spirits back with us," she explained.

"Do you really think that could happen?" Brian pressed.

"I don't think we should chance it," Marie said.

"Wouldn't it be cool if it worked, though? I mean, it would be proof that a supernatural realm exists! That's definitely worth whatever horror comes along with it," Brian argued.

"Are you insane?" Marie said.

"Don't you want to know if there is really something out there?" Brian asked.

"No," Marie snapped.

"Alright," Brian said. He slid his phone into his back pants pocket and held up his hands to ward off her anger. "You're right. This place is strange," he admitted.

Marie took Brian's hand and led him quickly through the remainder of the private Easter gown collection kept on display above Arnaud's French 75 Cocktail Bar in the New Orleans French Quarter. As they passed the final, blank-faced mannequin wearing a seafoam-green dress, the air conditioner kicked on blowing the fabric across Marie's bare arm. They looked at each other and gasped.

Matthew Schultz is the author of two novels: On Coventry and We, The Wanted. His stories "Black Friday" (Whale Road Review) and "On Foreign Shores" (The Birdseed) were both nominated for Best Microfiction of 2021.

The Dust Devil

by P. S. Nolf

I'm blowin' cross the plains to get ya. Hell's acomin' with me. Ya can't run from my ragin' red tower of brimstone. I'll whirl ya to the boneyard as souls of the damned scream. I kin spin those copper rivets right off the levis of them Monkey Ward cowboys till their chaps fall off. Toss any lost little doggies or dang eetn off the plains. Sand the spots off the pintos. Dare ya to grin. I'll scour ya phiz off.

Let's twirl a do-si-do, Lady of the Badlands, under this devil moon. We kin dance as I rain down dainty desert lilies for ya. Yellow Adder's Tongue, Naked Ladies, and Dimpled Dog Tooth. Then roll away to a half sashay.

Oh Trickster Coyote, we kin tell whappin' windies round the campfire. Smoke some devil's weed 'til we're whomper-jawed. Then get on our broncos to burn the breeze till dawn.

Goddess of Chaos, I kin make us some fine new hell stones to fling at the saddle bums. We kin funkify 'em to flusteration. Hootin' as we goes.

In the day, I fall to dirt an' dust 'neath the buckeroo bunks. This fluff has rows of sharpen' toothes. And a ten-gallon hat full of fingers and noses.

P. S. Nolf writes articles about horses, humor, and history for online and national journals such as Equus and Chatham University's Tributaries. Nolf is currently writing a narrative nonfiction book Raising Rough Riders in the White House: Roosevelt's Youngest Sons Archie and Quentin and their Pony Algonquin. In any spare time, P.S. is working on a MFA at Lindenwood University.

Bone Witch Hunt

by Elyse Russell

"There's power in a witch's bones."

That's what Teema's mentor had always told her, all those hundreds of years ago. It was why she now came out of her cave each new moon and hunted others of her kind.

Witches weren't rare; a garden-variety Cut Witch seemed to live in every other village. But Teema did not want to suck the marrow of a healer's bones tonight. No—what she wanted was another of her own sect. A Bone Witch.

Licking her thin lips, the spidery woman crept naked though the forest. The moon shone on her bald head and glinted on her talons whenever it peeked through the trees. She stopped to sniff, knowing that another Bone Witch had recently wandered into her territory.

Teema shivered with delight at the thought of cracking open a femur and absorbing its forces. Even each tiny finger bone was a sheer delight—a sweet pastry.

Following the trail, Teema lurched with each step, her gangly legs bending backwards, like a bird's, beneath her. She could see the light of a campfire up ahead, and could smell meat. A sharp crack sounded through the dark. The other witch had procured her own prey. Good.

Teema bared her fangs.

Elyse Russell is a writer of short stories and graphic novels. She has works accepted with: Mermaids Monthly, Crone Girl's Press, Quill & Crow Magazine, Outcast Press, HyphenPunk, and more. Her horror graphic novella, "The Fell Witch," will be released in 2022 with Band of Bards comics. Visit her website: elyserussellauthor.squarespace.com.

Lacrimal

by Julia Ruth Smith

When they took your sight I whispered about the
anatomy of your face although I was far from knowing
it well; the pleasure of your auburn hair in the wind,
wrapping around the dizzy heights of your cheekbones
and guttural laughter from ruby lips.

    I smoothed thumbs along the ridges of a lived-in
woman and purred the tip of my nose into bitter
crevices, smelling your journeys into spice and
wonder, the lust of other deluded men, the belief that it
was all over.

    I ran a sleek tongue around the edges of your orbit
finding the lacrimal bone; flicking with insistence to
see if you'd weep for us; if you would cry out my
name in the fizzing silence. I teased out the fragile
fingernail shape to displease you, caressing the crests;
still you were bone dry.

    You pleaded for music to interrupt our
wordlessness; let your head roll back in an ecstasy of
sorts and swayed in time to a past that I could never

know even if I loved you for a million tears. You cried then, fractured memories falling from the tiny pink shell in my palm; blind eyes scanning my face for a future; not trusting me to guide you there.

Julia Ruth Smith is a teacher, mother and writer who lives by the sea in Italy. She has been published by Sledgehammer Lit, Full House Lit, Versification, Zero Readers and others. She's on Twitter @JuliaRuthSmith1

Man of the Woods

by Alyson Hasson

"What was that?" Emma jumped.

"Just the wind. Keep moving," Mike snapped back at her.

They had been walking through the woods for what felt like hours. Emma wasn't sure when the realization occurred to her. Maybe it was after the fifth time they passed the gnarly tree that looked like an old man. But they were definitely lost.

"It's getting dark Mike, maybe we should come up with a plan here?"

"I can see that. I'm not blind. We just have to keep—" The echoing boom of thunder cut him off.

Before they could make another move, the sky lit in a blinding flare of lightning as it split the old man tree down. In a miasma of splintered bark and smoke, they were separated.

"Mike?!" Emma screamed. Her voice muffled by the wall of debris that now encapsulated her.

She stumbled forward, but the uneven ground

broke her balance and sent her toppling onto the ground. Brushing the dirt from her hands, she pushed herself up. Twisted branches and dried, crackling leaves surrounded her, barely visible in the dense fog.

She met the eyes of the gnarly old man, as a wide-sweeping grin covered his blood splattered face, now free of the bark tomb.

Alyson Hasson grew up in New Brunswick, Canada, where she obtained a love for nature-based horror. Her interest in horror movies, combined with her background in biology, spurred a curiosity that spurred her to write. She currently spends her days forecasting beer sales and her nights conjuring new monsters.

The Baykok
by Michael Stone

Allawa,

I'll be short. Can't use much ink.

You saw the lightning, didn't you? It came from your direction. A baykok came yesterday. I hope you were luckier than us.

A Runner, Gweden, came to town and bought 1.2 liters worth of rubber for Bagaangiti. *Liters!*

Gweden was set to rest and deliver the rubber come morning, but by night the lightning struck and a baykok screamed somewhere out in the forest. I locked the house up, but peered through one window I left unlatched. Gweden stood in the street, rapier drawn.

I could faintly see the black village, but the sound of the baykok's claws shredding the wall as it climbed was clear. It spotted Gweden and screamed. Suddenly it was on top of him, slashing at his sides. Gweden stuck his rapier underneath its chin, and it slumped over. His armor glinted in the moonlight, but I couldn't see the blood.

We spent 673 mL re-inking Gweden's equipment and the torn up walls. Half our income, gone.

Gweden's heading to Biiwaadena before

Bagaangiti, so I gave him 50 mL to deliver this to you. He returned the ink, saying: "She might not even get it."

I hope you were luckier.

Write back. Please.

Michael is a writer, born, raised, and living in Ottawa. When he's not working to survive, he's either writing or wasting his time away. He enjoys everything speculative, from science fiction, to fantasy, to surreal, to just plain weird. He's in the process of writing his first novel and mulling over drafts of the short stories he's collected over the years.

Beware the Witch in the Woods
by Hannah Smith

Trees adorn the twisting path, the light that filters through appears to dance and laugh.

The silence is broken only by the crunching of stones and the snapping of twigs as they twist and groan.

An idle crow swoops by ahead, cawing a warning and filling you with dread.

You sense the danger but cannot stop. The infernal pull makes your stomach drop.

You keep on walking, your end in sight, no-one around to witness your plight.

No-one around but she, the Witch whose spell you cannot break free.

You're drawing closer now, your heart begins to pound, your feet moving onwards through the forested ground.

Head screaming no but mouth making no sound, your body a puppet soon to be drowned.

The Witch extends her arms drawing you into an embrace, your death a reality you'll soon have to face.

She looks down upon you, her alluring face smiling, the look in her eyes is completely beguiling.

She kisses you softly upon your head and begins to unspool your sanity like a dangling loose thread.

The person you once were is dead and gone. The Witch once again begins her enchanting song.

Another innocent soul lost for good, beware beware the Witch in the woods.

Hannah Smith enjoys writing short horror and thriller stories. Hannah has been creatively writing since she was a child and is inspired by the horror and thriller books that she enjoys reading.

Skeleton in the Closet

by Cynthia McDonald

Amari touched her lips as Jack skipped down the steps. While she watched, the light from the streetlamp highlighted the sharp planes of his features. Her breath caught. She stumbled after him, reaching out to catch his hand.

"Come in for a drink?" she asked, her breath rising visibly between them.

His face crinkled into that one-sided grin. It had coiled heat in her all evening across the restaurant table.

"Absolutely—if you're sure."

"Yes," Amari said, tugging him behind her up the steps.

Warmth enveloped them as they stepped through her door. Amari pulled off her jacket and tossed it on a chair.

"Just put your coat there," she said. "I'll get us that drink."

Jack removed his jacket as she grabbed glasses

and ice.

She heard the closet open.

"No—" she cried out, turning, as Jack reached in to grab a hanger. She watched in horror as his body was jerked into the depths. He screamed.

The noises were unbearable. Amari sank to the floor.

The skeleton stepped out of the closet in its Jack suit. Bones gleamed wetly through skin in some places but as she watched, the damage healed itself.

Grinning, the skeleton said, "No more keeping me in the closet."

Cynthia McDonald is a disabled, bisexual, dog-loving mom of two kids in their 30s who still thinks she's 32 years old. She recently published her first YA novel, Drōmfrangil with Cinnabar Moth, LLC. Her short stories can be found in: The Highwire in YuzuPress, the anthology A Cold Christmas and the Darkest of Winters by Cinnabar Moth, the upcoming Bonemilk and SuicidAliens by GutSlut Press, and ToiletFlush 3 by Hellbound Books. She writes full time. She has brain cancer, but it does not have her.

In Church the Final Sunday

by Paul Wilson

Dee sat beside his hateful family. The preacher talked about remembering your blessings, but all Dee could remember was what it took to get here this morning. The screaming, crying, spilled food, and threats. Was this normalcy? Did everyone in the pews go through the same? It was madness. Why would anyone continue the torture? And not just getting to church, but every morning preparing for school and work, too.

He looked at his son, spoiled and playing with a toy Dee told him not to bring. He looked at his daughter lost on her phone. He looked at his shrew-wife. He watched them age, getting no better. He reflected in her glasses, growing old, older, dead, a corpse with staring sockets, slumped in the pew, molding away.

Fuck! This was his life? He remembered old girlfriends, paths ignored, opportunities wasted, all rail-roading him here with these life-eaters! They were grave dirt burying him. Was he expected to let them? Does a drowning man not have the right to save himself? Dee trembled. He had to act. How? Take that pen and stab his wife's eye? Snap the children's necks? Run?

"You are dismissed," the preacher said. *Yes!* Dee stood, Dee screamed, hoping to save himself.

Paul Wilson lives in a suburban neighborhood much like the one he turned into a horror playground in his novel Hostage. He lives with his wife, kids, and two cats. He has worked a spectacular list of jobs including retail district manager, a 911 operator, and the head of a college security department. You can follow him on Twitter: @Storydweller102

Under the Apple Tree

by H. S. Dilazak

— In loving memory of my dad.

Dear Diary,
Wednesday 15th Dec 21

Mum says it's confused. Christmas is nearly here, and outside the kitchen window the apple tree is waking up again. What does it mean…to have green foliage in December, like the summer I would never forget hadn't just come and gone? I know enough to know it's climate change causing confusion in the world; but when Mum left the house, I dug deep into the dark anyway—irrationally convinced there was something at work there that couldn't be explained by science.

I found his hand; the olive skin still holding onto the roots—just like he was holding my hand on the last day. I panicked and put all the dark back. I won't go out to the garden again; but, Mum will notice like she notices everything—only I can depend on us never talking about it.

Dear Diary
Wednesday 22nd Dec 21

When Mum was out, I dug and found his hair —
black, soft, thick—like it always was. His familiar
scent made it difficult covering it up again. Mum
keeps talking about him like he's still here; and I'm
wondering whether she does that because she knows
he's returning—piece by piece, under his apple tree.

*Halimah S. Dilazak was born and raised in
Birmingham where she currently lives. She writes
horror fiction often thematic of the surreal, mental
health, nature and social commentary. Her debut
gothic short story, "The Hollow" was printed in the
Winter 2021 issue of Quill and Crow Publishing
House; and her first flash fiction story 'The People in
the Boxes' has been published in Issue 7 by Bear
Creek Gazette for their 2022 anniversary issue. You
can find her on twitter @Dilazak_HS29*

Cold Hard Truth

by Vivian Kasley

From me to the cabin, it was nothing but deep white powder. I sunk into the Arctic quicksand as I attempted to escape the thing in the woods. Branches snapped as I fled and I could almost feel the steam from its rotten breath on the back of my neck. How was I to know? She was beautiful. Her voice as soft as her raven hair. The weekend was supposed to be discovering one another by the fire, but before I could remove my jacket, she'd taken my hand and said she wanted to take a walk. Hunger in her amber eyes that I mistook for lust.

And now, with death at my heels, my mother's voice echoed in my head. She hadn't taken to Constance the night I'd brought her to dinner. She wasn't impressed the way I'd been. Never judge a book by its cover, Ryan. It's what's on the inside that counts.

What used to be Constance let out a shriek that twisted my guts. My lungs were blistered with cold, but I kept going, hoping I'd make it to the axe I'd left on the porch before she sunk her teeth in.

"You were right, Ma," I wheezed. "You were fucking right."

Vivian Kasley hails from the land of the strange and unusual, Florida! She's a writer of short stories which have appeared in various science fiction anthologies, horror anthologies, horror magazines, and webzines. Some of her street cred includes Blood Bound Books, Silver Shamrock, Ghost Orchid Press, and The Denver Horror Collective. She's got more in the works, including a story in Kandisha Press's Slash-Her, a story in Vastarien, and poetry in Black Spot Book's inaugural women in horror poetry showcase: Under Her Skin.

We Eat Each Other

by Andy Cordoba

Seven watches Ines's body twitch and convulse, becoming an empty vessel now, a host only for the gooey thing that had been growing in her stomach for some time. Ines never told her, and Seven could only piece so much together. There was a lake Ines would go to after work, and Seven had always heard of the creature that lived at the bottom: a slimy, glistening thing that curled around itself and lured unsuspecting visitors to the depths. The moment their feet touched the edge of the water, their fate was already sealed. All an urban legend, Seven used to think. But not now that the painfully wet noise of Ines's excretion filled the empty space of their shared apartment.

Together, at last, after years of pretending. All a waste. Ines's abdomen breaks, cracking from the force of the expanding gooey thing. It seeps out from each tear, eating her skin. Ines cries, her voice giving out, now she's all hoarse and panting.

Seven stares at her, wide-eyed, and she holds Ines's hand tighter, it seems to be the only thing to do now. There's not much time left. The gooey thing, unsatisfied with the taste of Ines's stomach-skin, takes over her mouth, inching closer to Seven. One last kiss, before Ines falls over from the pressure, lips safely locked in a quick moment of trust.

Ines breaks it, chewing on Seven's tongue and tearing it out. Blood shoots out like bullets, splattering red on the bare bedroom walls they never painted. Ines and Seven's last communion, bloody copulation.

Andy is a horror/sci-fi writer and film critic based in Southern California. Their work often centers cyborgs, monsters, and themes of identity and disconnection. When they're not watching sitcoms with their cat Gus, Andy can be found writing reviews and essays for Hear Us Scream, or chatting with friends about vampires.

Desperation
by Erin Palmer

The fingerbones rattle in the little pouch. Small, so horribly small.

I try not to think of the way I got them.

My feet slap the wet pavement. Almost there. Soon I'll see him again.

Elaine's words force their way into my head. Never call on her in an act of desperation. Never. I push that thought aside.

The factory looms ahead in the dark. I claw my way up the fence and bolt through the yawning maw where the front doors had been. The statue is on the second floor. I run up crumbling stairs as quickly as I can.

It sits in what used to be an administrative office, in the corner, a looming, winged shadow. I can see hints of its features, and am grateful I can't see more.

I fall to my knees in front of it and dump the still-bloody fingerbones on the floor. I say the words, my voice trembling. For a moment, silence.

Then I hear movement downstairs.

I rush to the landing. The stairs are shrouded in shadow. But I can hear something coming up.

My heart pounds. "Derrick?" I whisper.

I can just barely see him now through the gloom.

Oh, God.

Oh, God, it's not him.

Erin Palmer is a writer of horror and dark fantasy. Her short fiction can be found in Tales to Terrify, The Wicked Library, Sanitarium Magazine, and Kyanite Press. When not writing she makes black metal music as Wolven Daughter and Dread Maw. She lives in Kentucky, and would like to meet a haint one day.

The Bone Tree
by Lyndsey Croal

The bone tree grows in the flowerbed at the end of our garden. It started off as a mushroom-like stump, before reaching upwards, branches twisting and hollow. When the wind blows, it makes a sound like a whisper.

The tree is different from the other plants. No leaves, and it smells funny—not sweet like daffodils, or fragrant like lavender, but musty like Daddy's old slippers. The ones Rowan used to steal and bury.

Nobody knows about the tree except Mama, Rowan, and me.

When Mama's sad, I hide by the bone tree. I feel safe there. Like if monsters came, its branches would curve outwards and wrap me in a hug. Then, I tell it I want to be a gardener when I grow up. Because I only ever feel properly happy in the garden.

Rowan joins me sometimes, though he usually gets bored and starts to tug at the tree's joints until he pulls a piece away. He runs into the house with it, brings back Mama to play. But she scolds him and returns the branch to the earth.

Maybe a new bone tree will grow from it. Though, if it were that easy, another Daddy would have grown in the flowerbed too.

Lyndsey is an Edinburgh-based writer and Scottish Book Trust New Writers Awardee. Her work has been published in a number of anthologies and magazines, including Dark Moon Digest, Shoreline of Infinity and Mslexia's Best Women's Short Fiction 2021. Her debut audio drama was produced by the Alternative Stories & Fake Realities podcast in 2021. Find her on Twitter as @writerlynds or via www.lyndseycroal.co.uk.

That's the Nuts of It

by Kai Double

"Are they . . . are they still out there?" Nora's breathing was chaotic and fast. It really made the whole atmosphere much worse, but nobody was going to call her out on freaking out. Not after what they had just escaped.

"I don't know." Tyler's response was practically a wail. He pressed hard against the gnarled board that separated the wine cellar, their hidey hole, from the outside world. He swallowed, thick glue-like saliva trickling its way down his throat, and held one eye against the crack in the board. For a moment it seemed like they might have been delivered a moment of reprieve. But, soon enough, Tyler spotted one.

It was feasting.

Feasting on Jerry's corpse, propped up against the battered fridge. It bit into his kidney and blood spewed out like a party popper. Tyler could make out it was one of those caramel bars. Vicious scavengers that hung around after something else had done the dirty work. A flash of their previous encounter, the white-chocolate fruit and nut buttons, Jerry's fingers dangling from its razor-sharp teeth, his nerve endings being slurped like noodles in a fleshy broth, danced darkly in Tyler's brain.

"Fuck! Why the fucking fuck is chocolate attacking?!"

Kai Double, a final year creative writing student, loves to take the usual and twist it into the downright blood-curdling! Mixing dark humour with visceral imagery, Kai likes to mix it up writing with both third and first person perspectives. Constantly submitting to all manner of flash fiction websites, magazines and competitions, Kai dreams of one day being a constant name in the word of flash fiction.

The Pursuer
by Craig Rathbone

The rain stung my face as I intensified my pace. I dared not look over my shoulder, I knew they were following me through the streets. I had picked her up back in the club, watching me from behind dark glasses. She seemed familiar.

I had been spooked back there but was now terrified as footsteps followed me into the alley. In the light of a neon sign, I saw two shadows, my own and another a few steps behind me. I panicked, breaking into a run for the end of the alley. I had no idea what lay beyond, but it had to be better than whatever fate awaited me here.

At the alley's end was a chainlink fence. Cornered, I turned to face my pursuer, hoping to fend them off or stun them long enough to push past. The person standing before me was very familiar: it was me.

My doppelganger saw the fear in my eyes and looked sad as she sunk the blade into my ribs.

"This gets no easier," she sighed, "but how else am I to pay my debt to the powers that be? If it's any consolation, you were doomed to achieve nothing anyway. Take my word for it."

Craig is a writer from Northwest England who was lucky enough to have three short stories published in 2021 alongside many talented fellow writers. He mainly enjoys writing fantasy and science fiction, enjoys gaming and movies and lives with his wife and his cat, Salem.

The Sand Approaches

by David Bowman

The sand approaches me and I step back, one, two, three. There are things in the water and I do not care for them. I cannot escape the sand and step back again. I can feel things crawling, crawling, crawling. What was that? Probably my imagination. I scratch and scratch and I cannot get rid of this goddamned itchy sand. I would tear my skin off if I could. The sand approaches me. I cannot leave this place. Was there ever any other place? I can't remember. The sea diminishes and the sand approaches me.

I can feel the sand in my veins; a scratching inside of my arms and legs. Every pulse slightly increases the itching. I taste the sand inside of my tongue. My throat grows raw with every single swallow of air. Oh god. Oh god, the sand is inside of my eyes. I can feel it with every blink. I breathe as shallowly as I can, but my lungs are filling with sand, rasping the air in my chest. I can feel my body eroding from within. Soon, the sand will be in my mind. My memories dissolve into nothing but sand. There is no more water. No more air.

Only sand.

David Bowman is a software developer and illustrator who lives in Indiana. His work has appeared in "Weird Horror" from Undertow Publications and "Field Notes from a Nightmare" from DreadStone Press.

They Called Him Egg Boy

by JR Santos

A small street under the cover of a bridge; the smell of garbage from the poorly kept bins that had their contents half spilled and the sound of cars a constant background droning noise as is for every city in every world known to us.

"Ugh, what's wrong with your head?"

It looked wrong, too big for any kid but especially this one because he was so small and skinny it made his head look even bigger.

One of the kids pushed him and the poor little egg didn't say a word and just fell over, landing head first. Everyone cringed at the noise and stopped laughing, because the noise was a crack so loud it echoed. They saw egg boy twitch as something dark and red pooled under his face, but the kid never made a sound; they had killed him, and no one would believe it had been an accident.

His big head cracked like an eggshell and the skin was so dry and brittle there were pieces falling inwards, as porcelain sounds echoed in the hollow which was so dark you could not see inside.

All the boys screamed as the hollow vomited. Little things hatched out of the egg boy's skull, hungry.

JR Santos is a Portuguese author who loves horror, creative creatures and so on! He's been writing for a while and you can find him on Twitter at @ccskeleton.

Bag Of Bones
by Ray Daley

I'm removing my bones, this is how I atone, For the sins in my life,

Let's begin with the skull, it's well, sort of a cull, for the death of a wife.

Moving down, take the spine, remove ribs, it's all fine (these are fibs) there is no pain,

Crack the arms, snap the chest, I simply can't rest, there's nothing to gain.

And then my left arm, there's no cause for alarm, After all, I deserve it,

Keep the right arm—it's needed, no warnings I've heeded, doing what I see fit.

With hips out the way, I can finally say goodbye to my legs and feet,

And then when they are gone, to the right arm I move on, My task here is almost complete.

This part is automated, I anticipated, that I couldn't reach,

With all bones removed, my life has vastly improved, no more sermons I'll preach.

My life was a noise, devoid of grace or poise, a torrent of din,

I'm feeling bereft, as now that is left, are organs and skin.

What's left of a man, I did all that I can, I'll soon be at peace,

While I may not be whole, I'm taking control, Of death's sweet release.

Ray Daley was born in Coventry & still lives there. He served 6 years in the RAF as a clerk & spent most of his time in a Hobbit hole in High Wycombe. He is a published poet & has been writing stories since he was 10. His current dream is to eventually finish the Hitch Hikers fanfic novel he's been writing since 1986. Tweet him @RayDaleyWriter

First Alternate
by Scott O'Neill

Naked, bound, and gagged, Serafina Lebedeva shivers despite the warm air in the warehouse.

It's warm for their comfort, not mine. Bastards.

Technicians and shamans bustle around her, building a pyre and chanting.

Endless skating around the track swallowed up my childhood. For what? Thick thighs, Osgood-Schlatter disease, and not-quite Olympic times in the thousand meter. Now this.

The pyre grows as shamans add carved sticks bearing athletes' names and place ritual bundles.

It's not even Team Russia this year and still they burn me for the Old Ones. Russian Olympic Committee. Same villains, different business cards.

The technicians withdraw as the sickly benzene smell of gasoline cuts through the incense.

The chanting crescendos. A shaman with a torch approaches Serafina. She cannot look away.

It's not fair. I worked as hard as anyone.

A breathless bureaucrat bursts into the warehouse. "Stop! Serafina is elevated to first alternate for speed skating. She must go to Beijing for the Olympics!"

Guilt chases relief across Serafina's features as they release her. They place Katya Zaytseva, first alternate sacrifice, atop the pyre.

Katya's wide eyes are full of tears.

Serafina flees the warehouse, heedless of her nakedness and the wintry Siberian air outside.

The chanting resumes. The flames roar.

Scott writes memos, emails, and briefing notes by day and speculative fiction by night. He lives in Kitchener, Ontario. He believes in true love, Murphy's Law, and prefers to assume incompetence before he assumes malice.

Pus Trickles Out Of My PS5 When I Turn It On And I Love It

by Stephen Arndt

Working as a linecook, with my baby Jaxsyn and babymama at home, meant no extra cash. I stopped shooting up for that baby girl. Since then my whole life's been itching something fierce. My choices: Get a PS5 or start shooting up again. Couldn't pay scalper prices. A man with no teeth sold me a modded Playstation for just a favor.

He made a disc outta me. Carved a circle out of the eagle tattoo on my left shoulder. Hurt, but not worse skin popping infections. He gave me two discs, tender dried up things that bled on my fingers. Told me he sells games behind the abandoned Tesco, for a price.

Worth it. Playing the damn thing was better than Fentanyl, like living the lives of the people those discs were cut from. That itch came back though, I needed more games. Babymama was confused when I tied her arm off, and gave her both shares of heroin. She was barely breathing when I dumped her out of the car behind the Tesco. I watched him play with her. Five new games, one less mouth to feed.

Twelve days till I was back at the Tesco with Jaxsyn. Told her we were gonna visit mama.

Stephen Arndt is the father of three young kids and writes in the slivers of time left. He is previously unpublished.

If Ever I was There

by Aaron E. Lee

I toss and turn each night, unable to settle my soul. My body writhes deep within, without sleep I'll be rendered un-whole. I learned why I am unable to sleep, my mind and body are not one. My mind swims the deepest fathoms, my body calls the earthly place home. Each joint, each sinew, each muscle sore, while my memories and fantasies collide. How can I heal myself when my astral body cries?

I've used crystals and acupuncture, dove into therapy and religion, but nothing has calmed these spirits within. I yearn for more than a basic life, I feel grounded, hostage of the Earth. I know there's more out there, but I must leave my body first. Life extends beyond vessel, as whine is poured from the bottle, I will break free of this chrysalis. Before I rot I'll... transform: Lepidoptera.

My new vessel will be light as air, lighter still, so I can travel on – onward and upward, and faster still, to the cold grey light of dawn. My future is brighter, lighter, and pure. To the distant horizon, where the sun blazes ever more. Those left behind will mourn, briefly but sincere, after long it will be asked if ever I was there.

Aaron E. Lee has three collections of short stories available on Amazon. Recently, he has been accepted into the anthologies, Remnants: Volume One, created by Stephen Coghlan, and 100-Word Horror: Beneath, edited by A.R. Ward. His work has also appeared in the blog at OrchidsLantern.com edited by C.R. Dudley, and on the Not Ready For Rhyme Time podcast, hosted by Taylor Woodland. You can read his blog at www.LeonianAmbitions.Wordpress.com.

Twitter @BOCArnie.

21 Months

by Judy Lunsford

"It's everywhere," the doctor said.

"What?" I asked in disbelief.

"We don't know how it spread so quickly, but it's everywhere," she said with tears in her eyes.

"What do you mean everywhere?" I asked.

It's really disturbing to have a doctor cry while giving me my test results.

I had spent the last week enduring MRI's, CT's, and bone scans of my entire body.

"So far, we have found it in your lungs, your lymph nodes in at least two places, and in your bones," she said. "I'm so sorry."

All I could think was "It's eating me alive. From the inside out."

"So, what can we do?" I asked.

She shrugged.

She friggen shrugged.

"There's a chemotherapy clinical trial that I think you might do well in," she said.

"Clinical trial?" I was stunned. "No surgery? No radiation?"

"Where would we stop cutting?" she asked. "And we can't radiate your entire body."

I was filled with horror and disbelief.

"How long do I have?"

"The people who have been in this clinical trial seem to do well for a while," she said.

"How long is a while?"

"The average length of time in the trial is 21 months," she said.

21 months to live.

Born and raised in California, Judy now lives in Arizona with her husband and Giant Schnoodle, Amos. She is a former library clerk and struggles with a chronic illness and is living with cancer. Judy writes mostly fantasy, but occasionally delves into other genres. She has written books and short stories for all ages. She likes playing RPG's and drinking lots of coffee.

Wish Tree
by Sarah Peploe

Down by the stream in the woods where he takes her every Tuesday afternoon, there is an old tree bristling with coins. Hundreds of them in serried rows and whorls. Some are shiny and new, some black as the earth beneath her cheek. They have been pressed partway into the trunk and left to poke boldly out showing half a hairdo or the furious face of a bird, or else hammered right down with a rock till they curl over. Every one is a wish, he tells her. He runs his hand over the trunk, enjoying their scaly resistance. Between the coins, the wood is damp and soft. You can push in easy, every time.

One Tuesday it amuses him to give her tuppence for the tree, although he himself is not superstitious, and particularly not when it comes to this type of cosmic begging. No. He is an abundantly satisfied man. So he is surprised when she, two foot shorter than him and a third his weight, takes him by his ankles easy as a doll and beats him against the tree again and again and again. Coins slice his cheeks, chip his teeth, split his eyes. He never did ask her what she wished.

Sarah Peploe's short stories have appeared in various publications including Mslexia, FlashBack Fiction, Snowbooks' Game Over, Martian Migraine's CHTHONIC, and Cursed Morsels' upcoming Antifa Splatterpunk. She also writes and draws comics as part of Mindstain Comics co-operative. She lives in York and tweets @SarahPeploe

Wear a Mask
by Cyndi Gradel

An awkward silence hangs over our kitchen table. Everyone is waiting for me to respond to my father's comments. My mother quietly fusses with her napkin. My sister glares at me with smug anticipation. Her husband continues to stuff his face with mashed potatoes.

"Fine," I say. "You want me to take off the mask, I'll take it off!"

I remove the blue disposable mask and place it on my lap. My father rolls his eyes and then scowls at my mother in disgust. My second mask is a red and green print cloth that I made myself. I slowly unhook it from my ears and pull it off.

My sister gasps and quickly pulls both hands to her face. Mom's eyes bulge as she shrieks in horror. A glass slips from my father's hands as he struggles to speak.

"What the…" he stammers. "What the hell is that?"

My mouth and jaw are covered in clusters of bumps filled with yellow pus. They look like a combination of smallpox and spider bites. I raise a hand to my chin to wipe away the ooze when one of them bursts open. I lock eyes with my father.

"Don't worry Pop," I say cheerfully. "It's not contagious."

Cyndi Gradel writes natural and supernatural horror. She has written for The Other Stories podcast. She is the creator of the podcast Stop Acting A Fool! She is a member of the Black Writers Collective. Cyndi lives and works in the Chicago area. @cyndigradel on Twitter.

The House

by Eddie D. Moore

The coroner stepped away from the hole in the wall and counted the small bones on the floor. "That should be all of them."

The Sherriff nodded. "Good. I hate getting called out here to run off thrill-seekers. This old house gives me the creeps. Let's get out of here."

The coroner watched the Sherriff and his assistant pack up the bones. He stared at the hole in the wall as they left the room. Dead silence filled the house. He glanced at the fingernail scratches on the boards they had removed to retrieve the child's remains.

"I don't know how long you were stuck in that wall before you died, but I hope your spirit can find some rest now."

The lights flickered, and a chill ran down the coroner's back. There was movement in the attic, and something fell out of the wall. A cat's eye marble rolled across the floor and stopped at the coroner's feet.

As he bent over to pick up the marble, a childlike voice whispered, "Play with me." Chill bumps in the shape of a small hand rose on the coroner's forearm.

After tripping over his own shoes twice, he ran down the stairs and out of the house.

When Eddie D. Moore isn't playing with his grandchildren, he is driving and visiting strange new worlds via audiobooks, or he is lost in his imagination writing his own tales. Pick up a copy of Poe-ish Tales Forevermore today! You'll be glad you did if you can sleep tonight.

That Woman
by Samantha Virginia

She was just like a sweater. Warm, comforting and if you pulled in exactly the right spot she'd come completely undone, leaving you exposed and cold.

I should know. I'd tugged on that particular string one too many times. Threadbare now, the nuts and bolts jangled together like a melody inside the the leather bag of her chest as she paced from left to right.

She was just like a factory. Sparks were her syllables and great, poisonous clouds of smoke rose from her mouth. Words stained her teeth and the ceiling. The bellows worked day and night inside that woman to produce the instruments of pain and claim the lives of men.

I, with my hammer in hand, sought out to be the organizer of the strike. But the line was broken like swells on a rocky shore.

She was just like a sea. A timeless beauty that

contained the raw material all poetry is fashioned from. Relentless and powerful enough to pull you under if you waded in too deep.

When I looked at her, I felt small and wept for my own mortality. Just like any river, mighty or humble, I came home, cursing and worshipping her name as I was dragged under.

Samantha Virginia is a writer from Minnesota with stories in the Horror and Sci-fi genres, currently published by Dark Fire Magazine and Manawaker Studios Podcast.

Ghosts Scream Eternal

by Alex Ebenstein

I died on my birthday.

The irony (besides the obvious) is how deathly terrified I was of getting old. Well, problem solved. Now I have a new problem: I'm stuck.

Is there an afterlife? I have a partial answer, I suppose. Heaven or Hell may yet exist, but I haven't made it so far. I'm cognizant, aware of my death (Slipped in the shower…really? How embarrassing), and I can see the people on Earth still living. I've seen others not of the living, but not like me either. One distinguishing feature separates me from them. Will I become the same in time?

I've tried talking to you, my dear, but you cannot hear, have not heard. I see your pain (oh, am I so vain?), your tears, your heartbreak. I hear our son wailing for me (since when did he care?). I cannot help you, though I wish nothing more (besides, perhaps, to still be alive). Had our life insurance applications been approved?

I don't know what to do. I have followed you, my

dear, for fear of losing you forever. But you've lost me already, haven't you?

If you hear (feel? sense?) this, just know there are no happy ghosts here.

Here, ghosts scream eternal.

Alex Ebenstein is a maker of maps by day, writer of horror fiction by night. He lives with his family in Michigan. He has stories published by Tales to Terrify Podcast, Boneyard Soup Magazine, and Cemetery Gates Media, among others.
Twitter @AlexEbenstein

Eve's Retribution

by Gemma Church

There is a tree of bones in my garden. Its trunk is formed of twisted femurs and spinal cords, the branches are conjoined radii, ulnas, tibias, and fibulas. Metacarpals form thousands of tiny twigs and its patella leaves sway gently in the breeze, floating to the floor when autumn comes.

It appeared many years ago. Just a small clavicle, poking out of the soil. I thought it was an animal bone as I plucked it from the ground and threw it onto the compost heap.

But the next day, the bone was back and growing from it was a tiny scapula and every time I plucked it from the soil, it grew back twice the size. So, I left it where it was, and watched it grow until my entire garden was in its shadow.

The plants all died. The birds no longer came. But the bone tree is not the scariest thing in my garden.

Because tonight I saw her crawling from the boney roots. She edged along the bare earth and tapped the window with her phalanges fingertips.

"Adam," she rasped, "come take a bite of my apple."

And she held aloft my beating heart. I had no choice but to take a bite.

Gemma Church lives in rural Cambridgeshire and is a freelance science and technology copywriter. She recently gained a Diploma in Creative Writing at Cambridge University and is currently studying with the Faber Academy.

With This Ring
by Tom Deady

When the severed finger arrived in the mail, it was just another day for Max Penn. His fans had been sending him crazy shit ever since his horror novel became a best seller. Then he noticed the ring on its finger. The ring he had given his ex-girlfriend right before he dumped her. The ring he gave all his girlfriends right before he dumped them.

He picked the finger up with two of his own. It felt real, and the part that used to be attached to a hand was gross enough to be real. In fact, the blood still looked wet. And did the finger feel…warm? "You're crazy, Penn," he muttered.

He stared at the finger, trying to see if he could recognize who it had belonged to. He giggled when he realized how all fingers looked alike. He supposed he should really call the police. He dropped the finger back into the box then examined the package. He frowned when he realized it was just his name and address, no postage.

He opened the front door and noticed the drops of what looked like blood on the porch. Then Jenny stepped out from behind the bushes holding hedge clippers, her stump still dripping blood.

Tom Deady's first novel, HAVEN, won the 2016 Bram Stoker Award for Superior Achievement in a First Novel. He has since published several novels, novellas, and a short story collection. Tom has several publications, including the sequel to Eternal Darkness coming out in 2022. He has a Master's Degree in English and Creative Writing and is a member of both the Horror Writers Association and the New England Horror Writers Association.

The Horror of Oz

by K. J. Shepherd

When I first saw Dorothy I thought she was quite mad. What drove her like that? What made her stalwart in her efforts to get back home, even though I'm certain her "home" didn't exist? When I first saw her singing like she was, down that damned brick-road, I was certain she was the crazy one. And they say she has a brain?

Well, had.

It's so odd how it pulsates. Even now, in my straw hands.

Tinny was easy enough to convince. Clanking around without a heart for his whole life, then she practically falls into our laps.

It was a mercy, you see. She was so ill. Talking of places that didn't exist. Couldn't exist.

Lion wasn't so easy. But his corpse next to hers was the price he paid for getting in the way. Huh. I guess he did find his courage in the end. All we had to do was rip apart that little thing that was with her. She called it a dog, I think. Didn't look like any dog I ever saw, even the insides were different.

"Is this it?" Tinny asked.

I nodded. Tinny opened his chest and plopped the red mass inside him.

And it began to pump.

Kyle grew up mostly in Texas and is, unfortunately, still there. He spends his days reading and writing (though never really enough of either), playing video games, listening to death metal, and hanging out with his daughter, Harper. He daydreams about how cool he'd look in various hats.

206 Words

by Morton R Leader

So, I saw this challenge, to write a short horror story using only two hundred and six words.

That's not easy, I've written short stories, I've written novels of thirty-five to seventy thousand words, across different genres, but two hundred and six!

I mean why, it's crazy, I just couldn't get my head around it. Was it even real?

Anyway, I like horror, so I sat and thought about it. It needed a twist, that was for sure.

Demons, Zombies, slashers, aliens, monsters, folklore—ideas came and went, but the length defeated me, it was just too short. How was I supposed to build a picture, the set-up, the characters arc and finally a killer twist?

This was driving me insane, not only the story but why had I seen it, was it fate, the lady that had sent it out seemed nice, I'd seen her on Twitter, she had like one of my tweets.

Who is she, was I being messed with?, I hate being messed with, why choose me?

It's a set up I'm sure, I can literally see her now,

standing in her kitchen, laughing at me, her house wasn't too hard to find after all. That back gate needs mending.

Morton has written several books, all available on Amazon including 'History is a Lie' and 'The Liar, the Bitch, and the Warmonger' and he is a big supporter of the indie publishing scene. Find him on Twitter: @LeaderMorton

Happiness of the Whole World

by Jacob Ian DeCoursey

Our ceremony completed, Camilla and I lie in the snow a while. Flurries cascade from the looming gray dawn overhead. My body grows colder.

Blood and snow mix into a red slush. Camilla's blood or mine? Maybe both.

I turn to Camilla, holding her guts in with shaking hands. We're going to die?

"Eventually," she says.

No. Here, like this.

Camilla produces a cigarette stained with burgundy fingerprints, draws a lighter.

One strike. Two strikes. She doesn't bother with a third. The cigarette drops into the snow.

Twigs snap.

A caravan of masked figures step out from behind the trees. On their heads, crowns of sticks bend and curl like tendrils. Atop each crown rests a familiar sign.

Tattered robes of sackcloth, the color of spring dandelions, hang open draped over their gaunt shoulders. Otherwise, these necrotic bodies shamble forth naked in the icy wind.

We'd summoned them: actors in that forthcoming play of lost gods, claiming the earth as their rightful stage—

The long-waiting shepherds of our King in Yellow.

They press on, indifferent to our presence.

I thread my fingers between hers.

Did we secure happiness for the world?

She grins, eyes wide and jaundice.

"It's not that simple, Cassie. Nothing ever is."

Jacob Ian DeCoursey was born and raised in Maryland. He's a master's degree dropout and "essential worker" laboring too many hours for too little pay. Since 2007, his writing has appeared in numerous publications (many now defunct) both online and in print. Reflex Press has longlisted his flash fiction for their quarterly international competition. In 2019, during a stint of unemployment, he released his first book, Vivid Greene: and Other Unusual Stories. IG: @billy_collins_in_hell

Teeth of a Traitor

by Emily M. Dietrich

"My boy," Teresa cries, wading through the costumed revelers. "Has anyone seen my boy?"

A sob chokes her throat and her eyes strain against the dying light. She bumps into a pint-sized witch, and the girl stumbles. Parents shout, but Teresa is already pushing between a pack of pumpkins. Her panic-induced tunnel vision sees only bobbing heads and sugary smiles and too many children to count.

But none of them are her little ghost.

He didn't even want to be a ghost. The stained sheet was so unfair, but she couldn't afford anything. Not after the divorce. Her ex took everything, and now he took the boy.

Where is he?

Her heart constricts as she breaks into a run.

How could he steal this too?

Her chest quakes with pain.

There.

Tears pour down her cheeks, but she sprints.

Under the tree.

Teresa rips back her ex with force she didn't know she had. Hunger shreds her insides.

"You left me with nothing." She rasps at him but falls to her knees before the boy.

"You don't get the child too." Her voice turns feral.

"He's mine." She cups the child's mouth so he can't scream.

"One last bite." She purrs.

And Teresa sinks her teeth.

Emily M. Dietrich is a technical science writer by day and a speculative fiction writer by night. Her short story "Alterity" won first place in the Writer's Digest Popular Fiction Awards for Science Fiction / Fantasy. She can be found at emilymdietrich.com or on Twitter @emilymdietrich.

Her Whispers
by Anna Strand

I hear her whispers in the walls. Her bones chatter and creak as the winter wind blows through the house, the air whistling as it passes through the dark crevices of her abode. Only I hear her whispers. They are near-silent, blood curdling shrieks that pierce through the veil and slit open my ears, but only I am deigned to hear them. Her whispers, a soft caress against my ear from her hand of enmity, are only meant for me.

It was an accident. She never understood that—she's never forgiven me—but I swear it was an accident. She hasn't left me since.

Every night, I lie in bed listening to her. I ask if others can hear her—hear the creak in the wall—but only I ever do. I have attempted to run, to hide, from this house and these haunted walls, but the sound never leaves me. It rings in my ears, following and hounding me no matter how far I flee.

I have long forgotten the amity of silence. I hear her voice always, sometimes it is all that I hear. She won't let me forget her; I cannot be free of my guilt.

Every night, I hear her bones sing.

Anna Strand is a college student and aspiring writer. In between classes, she can often be found reading a book or writing stories on her cellphone.

The Wedding Gift

by Michele Cacano

Ben leaned away from the monstrosity. "It's horrifying."

Maura twitched. "It's the thought that counts."

"Dear God, what thought?" Ben shuddered. "I thought your grandmother liked you."

"It's a family heirloom. From the old country."

"Is the old country Hell?"

"Stop!" Maura slapped Ben's shoulder. She placed the cuckoo clock on the mantel. Red-painted cornices on crackled ivory, two feet high, and covered in grinning dog-headed men. "Gargoyles are protective. Good luck, right? Scares away evil?"

"Then get a mirror, because that is the evilest thing I've ever seen."

Maura took his hand. "Come to bed, Husband."

"Yes, Wife." Ben smiled.

Hours later, Maura woke, alone, to dissonant chimes. "Ben?"

She went to stoke the fire. There stood Ben, stiff and slack-jawed. Light flowed from his mouth to the carved creatures in the open clock doors. Maura tried to make sense of it. "Ben?"

Ben strangled a reply. His fear-filled eyes shot sideways, towards Maura. The light appeared to be something from inside Ben, being sucked out. Each chime reverberated louder, rattling her bones. With the last, darkness. Ben crumpled to the floor.

"What was that?" Maura screeched.

Ben slowly unfolded himself, sat upright, and turned to Maura. "What was what, dear?"

Michele Cacano is an artist, writer, and massage therapist in Seattle. She writes horror, fiction, nonfiction, memoir, and poetry. Both mystical and skeptical, she loves challenging norms and bridging distances, be they physical, mental, or metaphysical. Follow on Twitter and InstaGram @MicheleCacano.

Porcupine Man
by Reed Beebe

Dave noticed the abandoned comic book on the bench just as his bus arrived; with no one else around to claim it, he picked it up and boarded. The bus was vacant, except for the driver; Dave took a seat at the back. Settled, he inspected his treasure.

The comic featured "Porcupine Man"; Dave was not sure about the character's name or the comic's title, as the letters were foreign (almost, but not quite, like Japanese kanji), so Dave dubbed it, because the main character was an obese naked man covered in quills.

The artwork was rough, uncolored illustrations with red and black ink that didn't align well, creating a discomfiting visual effect. The protagonist was either a monster or a superhero – he ran terrified through a gothic city, yelling at other terrified characters via indecipherable word balloons – shooting endless quills out of his body that tore into bystanders with gruesome effect. Eyes were gouged; red ink stained clothes and concrete. Also, random giant wasps picked up pedestrians and bit off their heads.

It was a strange comic.

Dave disembarked with the comic and walked

home. When he opened the door, quills destroyed his eyes as a waiting porcupine man screamed words Dave would never understand.

After years spent battling monsters and solving mysteries, Reed Beebe has retired to a quiet village to write fiction. Reed's work has been published by AHOY Comics, DC Comics, and Soteira Press. Reed also blogs about comics at medium.com/meanwhile.

Homegrown
by Eric Netterlund

Lacy stopped washing her breakfast dishes. Through the kitchen window— a substantial green mass writhed in the dirt in the garden out back. She'd seen the reports and shaky videos of green tentacles sprouting in backyards and community gardens.

"Anders?" Lacy called. "Have you been outside this morning?"

"No. Could take a walk later if you'd like," her brother said.

"There's something in the garden. Something big."

"I'll take a look later," he said.

Lacy placed her bowl in the drainer, and grabbed her things. She had to get out of the house for a little bit. "I'll be back for lunch— just going to drop by the office quick."

The house was empty at lunchtime. The only thing that was different from any other day was the solid stalk colonizing their garden. It hadn't changed since the morning.

Anders was gone.

The pod started growing a week later. By July it was almost three feet long and trembled in the sunlight.

Lucy cleared a layer of leaves off of the pod, as the October moon cast the pod's shadow over her shins.

Her stomach clenched. Another night waiting. Praying that when the pod opened, maybe she could have what was left of her family back.

Eric Netterlund writes short quiet horror and weird stories from his attic in Minneapolis. He returned to the frozen north after seven years in Colorado, and he misses the mountains but loves the lakes. You can find him on Twitter @ericnetterlund.

Florae

by Maxwell Marais

I can feel it moving beneath my skin.

It started with the coughing—a thick, moist, viscous sort of coughing, a phlegm lodged in the back of my throat that never came up. And then when it finally did, as I bent stooped over the sink, grasping its edges with a white-knuckled grip, I saw a small yellow and shriveled leaf hit the bottom of the basin. And then I knew. I had not gotten out of the expedition unscathed. When we first got back we were sure Edwards had been the only one infected. He was quarantined immediately, and we wrote ourselves off as safe. But then others started disappearing, breaking off contact, and I'd always had a lurking suspicion…

And now it's here. In me. I can feel it when I breathe, little stems and leaves brushing my esophagus, roots bundled in my sinus cavity. I'd thought the headaches the latter caused were the worst of it – awful, spiking things that left my head reeling and my vision starred with oil-spill colors. But now, as I look into the mirror, I can see plant matter pushing through my tear duct, can feel it behind my teeth. And now I'm certain.

Soon, it will bloom.

Maxwell Marais is an author, artist, and musician living in Montreal, Canada. When they aren't frantically scrawling down the weird fiction and horror that crawls out of their brain, they can be found attempting to summon (with limited success) horrible abominations from beyond our world.

They Don't Love You Like I Do
by Alejandro Gonzales

They don't love you like I do, Jim. Your parents, your friends, your teachers; they'll never get inside your head like I have.

I've seen your fantasies, watched your most intimate moments from another realm and been a phantom shoulder to cry on. If only you could hear me.

So many years spent in this void watching them abuse you. Yet, the other day, I could feel. I could reach into the mortal world and enjoy your warmth, sweetheart.

You may not be aware of my existence, but I know everything about yours. The foods you prefer, the way you like the crust cut off your sandwiches even though your girlfriend doesn't think it makes a difference, the movies you really want to watch even though you suffer through those actions flicks for your father's sake.

It wasn't my choice to fall in love with you, but I did, and I think that very love is setting me free, allowing me to figuratively and literally feel once more.

Soon I will be able to do what I've been waiting to for so long. Everyone you think loves you must go. I'm coming, my love. And when I do, there will be nobody to stand in between us.

Alejandro Gonzales is a horror writer living in Northern California. His works can be found in magazines such as Trembling With Fear and The Drabble.

Something Broken

by Steven Sheil

There was something broken inside Laura. It has been that way for almost a year now, ever since she had found her mother newly dead on her kitchen floor, her thin lips drawn back over her teeth in a pained grimace, her rheumy eyes bulging out from their sockets, as though being pushed from behind. As the grief and terror of the moment had hit her, Laura had turned away, her shuddering hands fumbling at the keys on her phone, and so in that moment she had missed seeing her mother's lifeless head tilt and the left eyelid twitch as the broken thing emerged from the scabbed-over hole behind her mother's ear, and began to scuttle its way across her face, its many thick legs making dimples in the whitening skin before dropping silently to the floor. The numb grief that enveloped Laura prevented her from even feeling the incision that the broken thing's tiny claws made in the back of her skull, and by the time she was talking to the emergency services it had burrowed its way completely inside her.

And now it sat there, the broken thing, as it had

done ever since, slowly, methodically breaking everything inside Laura, piece by tender piece.

Steven Sheil is a writer and filmmaker from Nottingham, UK. His work has previously appeared in Black Static, The Ghastling and as part of the Black Library anthologies Invocations, The Harrowed Paths, and The Accursed. He is also co-director of Mayhem Film Festival.

Brainwave Corpse

by Steven Bailey

The two women sat, and each promised themselves not to be the first to speak. The office was dark and streamlined and it smelled of lemon disinfectant. The older woman was still. The younger felt her leg bounce against the desk and she had to try not to vomit. The speaker waited. The older woman had paid for three words. Any more cost at least a month's wages.

"We can't do this," said the younger woman. "It's not right."

"Look," said the older. "It's turning on."

A white light grew from the base of the speaker. Then, a voice.

"You are Miss Mary Maiden and Mrs Joanna Maiden. Confirm," it said.

"Confirmed."

"Yes. I mean, confirmed."

"The deceased is Mister John Maiden. Confirm".

They did.

"You have paid for three words. The Crad Champion Corporation has reanimated the final brainwaves for you. Please enjoy. Final brainwaves of the deceased are as follows:"

"Oh God," said Mary. "No."

"He was a good man. He loved life. He deserved company at the end," said Joanna.

They looked at the speaker.

"Thank God," it said. "Finally. Thank God, finally. Thank God, finally. Thank God, finally."

Mary felt her hands turn cold and Joanna cracked open inside.

Steven Bailey is an emerging freelance and creative writer from Northern England. He enjoys the written word so much that if he's not writing the written word, he's reading it, or writing about how to write the written word. If you need him, simply speak out loud about Ernest Hemingway or time-travel, and he will probably arrive unannounced.

Re: Onboarding
by Avery Parks

Congratulations on beginning your second life! Welcome to the team. This may not have been an outcome you considered when donating your body to science, but rest assured that many of our team members appreciate this exciting opportunity.

Here at <redacted>, we prioritize high-level user experience. In your new role, you'll help us to drive engagement and increase growth. Second life labor is opening up new doors for the formerly-dead to continue contributing to society, and we're sure you're eager to get started. Your life may be limited to your cubicle, but don't be afraid to think outside the box!

You may find certain changes to your body disturbing, which is why we allow for a three hour acclimatization window. Feel free to use this time to explore your cubicle and reacquaint yourself with the structure and movement of your body. (Side effects of reanimation may include, but are not limited to: dry mouth, peeling skin, unusual urges and cravings, and feelings of existential dread.)

Remember, your body no longer requires rest, so we hope you enjoy this opportunity to give this job your all. Any attempts to leave your cubicle will be met with immediate disciplinary action.

Congratulations once again, and welcome aboard.

Sincerely,

Management.

Avery Parks is a SFF writer of short fiction. Her work can be found at Cossmass Infinities and MetaStellar Magazine. She lives in Texas with her family, a variety of pets, and (according to some) too many books. You can find her on both Twitter and Instagram at parks_writes.

Mother

by M.T. Rightman

"No, you've had enough candy today, James. Go play outside and I'll call you when dinner is ready."

That was the sentence that set eight-year-old James to brooding on his swing in the back yard. His mother was mean.

Angrily, he glared at the cracked concrete before him. His father told him to always walk over the cracks, never on them. Step on a crack, it'll break your mother's back, and there's 33 bones in the human back, son, so gotta protect your mom. He could still hear his father saying that to him.

He walked up to the crack, thinking.

"James, dinner is about ready, come in and wash up for dinner."

He looked at his mother standing in the back door.

"Can I have candy for dinner?"

"No, we've been over this. Now come on."

She turned to go, and as she did, James jumped with both feet onto the crack in the concrete. He heard a crunch and a scream as his mom toppled to the ground. She looked at her son, pain and fear in her eyes.

Another jump. More screams, another crunch.

"I'll jump again if you don't give me candy."

"STOP!" his mother cried.

"Okay, 31 more jumps to go."

M.T. Rightman is a horror author living in Chicago, IL, with his husband T.W. They sometimes team up for the occasional short story. M.T. is the author the novel, BABS' DINER, the short story collection GAMBLING WITH THE DEAD AND OTHER SHORT STORIES, and has several pieces in other anthologies. Find him on Twitter: @mtrightman.

How I Turned My Little Brother Human
by D. Matthew

The air went bad and everyone fell asleep except mama and me.

For a while it was just us two, drinking the river, eating whatever came up. Nice, quiet. Then mama said she had another me in her tummy.

"I don't know how it happened," she said. "A miracle from God." I never met God but mama always said how he gave us miracles, the sun and stars and all.

Mama's tummy grew and grew. I brought her river water when her head got hot.

One day mama screamed and I got so scared I fell down. When I got up, mama was asleep and my little brother was born. He wasn't human yet. Just a lump, no arms or legs or nothing, lying all gray and bloody on the floor.

I rolled him to the river and cleaned him up. I stuck in sticks for arms and legs, black stones for eyes, white stones for teeth. Green leaves for hair, red flowers for lips.

I took him back home and sat him in a chair next

to mama. "Look, mama," I said, "a miracle. Our baby's human now."

"Buzz buzz," said the flies on her lips. What I think that means is, "Thank you, sweetheart."

D. Matthew Urban grew up in Texas and now lives in Queens, New York, where he reads weird books, watches weird movies, and writes weird fiction. His stories have appeared online from Black Hare Press. He can be found on Twitter at @breathinghead.

The Call
by Kim King

My friends finally convinced me to go see this live band in a pub—some cover band or other. It's loud, bustling and oddly comforting. At one point a particularly heavy song comes on and my friends push me to the centre of an impromptu mosh pit. Warm bodies bashing against one another, pushing, shoving, stumbling.

When the song ends I get out of it and decide to call it a night. I feel I'm a little old for moshing now. As I reach for my phone to call a cab, I find it's not in my pocket—did it fall out or get pinched in the pit? I search every pocket and potential nook and cranny I may have put it in, as well as tables and the floor.

My friend gives me their phone to ring it. On the second try, someone picks up. I can just make out heavy breathing and some giggling then they hang up. They don't answer any more calls.

My friend calls me a cab and I start thinking of how I can contact my provider to block the phone. I get home. It's late. I'll go online tomorrow.

In my bedroom, on the bedside table, lies my phone.

Kim is from Birmingham, currently living in Armitage. Watching popular sci-fi and fantasy programs when she should have been watching CBeebies gave her a deep knowledge base, which she draws upon with her writing. An amalgamation of everything she has seen and read creates rich stories, believable character decisions and convincing scientific explanations whilst keeping the characters at the heart of every story.

Visitors

by Fionnuala Meehan

Inagh felt the cold grip of fear crawl along her spine and clamp her heart. The familiar low vibration rattled her bed, and the curtains shuddered in symphony.

It was back, outside.

Robotically, she rose.

Slowly.

She had no control over her body. She didn't want to move but it did as it pleased. The hem of her nightie slipped to the floor and her feet moved slowly, one in front of the other.

'Stop, please,' she begged. 'Go back to bed.'

Moving towards the window.

'No.'

Inagh watched as her hand grabbed the curtain and pulled it back. Her heart was beating fast. She knew what was on the other side.

The vibration grew louder, penetrating the room, demanding her attention.

She tried to look away, tried not to see.

She trembled, it hovered.

Cold fingers tap, tap, tapping.

Her eyes locked on the familiar figure. A statue of her mother floated at her window. Eyes set in stone, staring at her.

Expressionless.

Dead.

She looked into the dark night beyond, to the army of statues making their way to her window.

She was terrified. There had never been so many.

They were coming for her and there was nothing she could do about it.

Fionnuala has attended many creative writing courses over the years and is an active member of a local writing group. When not writing, Fionnuala is busy raising three book-devouring readers.

Knock, Knock, Knock

by Keith Cashin

Knock once.

Knock twice.

Knock thrice.

They come in the dark. They come in the light. They come.

The man sits at the piano, his fingers running over the keys. A sad melancholy tune echo's off the empty ballroom walls.

Changing key he hears the three knocks as the door swings open, they have arrived.

Taking their positions around the room, they bow to their partners and clasp hands.

Hidden violins play, the cello moans, the man moves his bony fingers to deeper keys.

The guests begin to sway around the empty ballroom.

The music builds as they sway and dance.

The old lamps burst into light, the murky damp walls are replaced with fresh paint, the decrepit chandelier rises off the floor and flickers to life.

They dance and they dance.

Their faces masked with pain, translucent figures spin faster and faster, the music building and building to the crescendo.

The man at the piano runs his fingers over the keys with lighting speed, his brow slick, his black eyes blind to all but his task.

The violins screeching behind him as they reach the peak, the guests no more than a blur, then silence.

It stops, they leave.

Knock once.

Knock twice.

Knock thrice.

Keith Cashin is a writer from Ireland. He's been writing or making up stories for as long as he can remember. Most of his work currently consists of short stories, but he is on the second draft of his first book. He enjoys chatting with other writers or readers. You can find him on twitter @cashin_keith or Instagram @keith_cashin_writing.

Bones

by Jacek Wilkos

"Did you know the human body has two hundred and six bones?"

He opened his eyes. Consciousness came slowly, as did the sharpness of vision. Dark shapes took human form. Two men dressed in black stood in front of him. Masks hid their faces.

He tried to get up but couldn't move. Looked down and realized he was tied to a chair.

"Who are you?! What the hell is going on here?!"

"Did you know the human body has two hundred and six bones?" one of the men repeated with the same dispassionate voice.

"So what?"

"How many of your son's bones did you break?"

The man tied to the chair turned pale as the masked one continued.

"Phalanges, radius, tibia, collarbone, ribs..."

"It's not like that, I..."

"Yeah, yeah. We know the story. He fell down the stairs, off his bicycle, didn't see the cupboard, and so on. Save that bullshit for the doctors, teachers, social workers. We know the truth."

The other man pulled closer a rolling table filled with various tools.

"What... what are you going to do?"

"Exactly what you think. We'll break your bones. We've got a whole two hundred and six to choose from. So, which one do we start with?"

Jacek Wilkos is an engineer from Poland. He's addicted to buying books. He loves black coffee, dark ambient music, and riding his bike. His stories are published in numerous anthologies including: Black Hare Press, Alien Buddha Press, Eerie River Publishing, Insignia Stories, Fantasia Divinity, Reanimated Writers Press, & KJK publishing.

That Song Again
by Epiphany Ferrell

She called it "our song." I hated it even then.

I've heard it every night for a week now, creeping up through the floor, oozing through the walls.

She's in my living room, seated at my piano, and she's playing that song. She looks just like she did in 1982. Except now she's opaque. Her fingers dissolve as they touch the keys, as she plays that song over and over, making the same mistake every time, hitting the same wrong note.

It was a car wreck. Post-prom. She was beautiful and cold and virginal. I was drunk and an asshole. I haven't thought of her for years. It must be the anniversary of her death, a date you'd think I'd know but which I've spent a decade trying to forget.

We were quarreling when we went off the road. I was making reckless promises about loving her forever if only she'd let me that night. She was going to relent. If I'd love her forever, she said, if I'd swear on my eternal soul. I promised, of course.

I made promises at her grave, wild with remorse, promises forgotten before the grass grew on her grave.

The music stops. She turns her head. And speaks.

Epiphany Ferrell lives perilously close to the Shawnee Hills Wine Trail in Southern Illinois. Her stories appear in more than 50 journals and anthologies, including Pulp Literature, Unnerving Magazine, The Sirens Call, Predators in Petticoats anthology, and other places. She is a two-time Pushcart nominee, and won the 2020 Prime Number Magazine Flash Fiction Prize. Follow her on Facebook or Twitter, or learn more at epiphanyferrell.com.

Heaven or Bust
by Christopher Henckel

Purgatory was nothing more than an airport lounge with excellent lighting. Heaven's Pearly Gates occupied the first terminal, flanked by St. Peter. The other terminal dead-ended in a port-a-loo style pit. I've never been one for ecclesiastic woo-ha, but this was a no-brainer. Heaven or bust.

The celestial self-service kiosk asked if I'd coveted my neighbor's wife, failed to keep the Sabbath holy, or committed adultery? Yikes.

I selected no to all.

A pop-up appeared: You've omitted ten sins. Please review and confirm.

I jerked my hand back, half a heartbeat from a coronary. I took a deep breath, then carefully selected the edit button.

The pop-up disappeared, and the screen changed: your confessions have been recorded. A roaming attendant will escort you to your final destination. The kiosk spit out a bag tag with Hell printed on it. At the same time, the crowd parted, and a Dark Angel made his way toward me.

Yikes! Not what I had in mind.

In the opposite direction, I glimpsed St. Peter standing beside the Pearly Gates. He had the build of a NFL linebacker, but I reckoned I could take him. So, I tucked my chin and charged, dropping anyone in my path.

Heaven or bust, baby.

Born in the backwoods of West Virginia, Christopher Henckel is a country boy down to his molecular structure. He now lives in New Zealand where he works for the Government as a Senior Procurement Specialist. Christopher was a finalist in the Writers of the Future Contest (2020) and Semi-Finalist (2021). He was the third-place winner in the Mike Resnick Memorial Short Story Competition (2021), and his short story Echoes of Gliese was published by Galaxy's Edge Magazine in their January 2022 issue.

https://www.christopherhenckel.com/

Under the Canal
by Caitlin Marceau

Marilis hates crossing the frozen canal. But with the bridge down and her grandmother helpless, it's the only way across. Still… she knows what's waiting for her in the black water. She takes a deep breath and steps onto the ice, eyes focused on the other side as she moves. She doesn't look down.

Never down.

When she's halfway across, it starts like it always does: banging, screaming, nails dragging across the underside of the ice. She ignores it, moving faster across the slippery canal until she trips, crashing onto the cold surface.

His eyes look up at her from the water, wide with fear as he desperately bangs his fists against the ice, trying to break out. His panic, his blue lips, the water soaking his jacket and pulling him down; it's exactly how her brother looked when he fell through the canal almost five years ago.

Marilis wants to help. She wants to smash through the ice with her bare hands and pull him out. Just once she wants to save him.

But she doesn't.

She gets up, eyes fixed on the trees, and crosses

the canal. The monster wearing her brother's face will still be there when she gets back.

It always is.

Caitlin Marceau is an author and lecturer living and working in Montreal. She holds a B.A. in Creative Writing, is a member of both the HWA and the Quebec Writers' Federation, and spends most of her time writing horror and experimental fiction. She's been published for journalism, poetry, as well as creative non-fiction, and has spoken about horror literature at several Canadian conventions. Her debut collection, Palimpsest, is available from Ghost Orchid Press and her second collection, A Blackness Absolute, is slated for publication later this year. For more, check out CaitlinMarceau.ca.

Hunter-gatherer
by Dan Godley

"How do you know which ones are safe to eat?" He kicked his boot into the lifeless corpse and sniggered to himself. The body was cold and responded as enthusiastically as a bag of sand left out in the rain.

"Look at the tongue. If it's got red spots or green gunk on it, you should stay clear." The words read out like a script. She was sick of saying them.

"What if they don't have a head."

"They all have heads."

"This one doesn't." He picked up his shovel, wielded the handle with both hands extended above his head, and ploughed it through the neck. It went in at an angle and seemed to get caught around the shoulder blade as it slammed through the flesh. She wasn't amused as she watched.

"They were people, you know. Same as me and you. They suffered the same way we suffer. Probably more. Have you seen 'em when they start to get ill?"

"Fuck 'em. They're disgusting. I'd rather not eat." He was trying to pull his shovel out by putting his boot on the half-severed head. They could hear the bones crushing as he struggled.

"Seen this?" she said, swinging her shovel straight into his cheek.

Dan Godley is a blogger from Cheshire. His blog, Ebb and Flow, was started after receiving an unexpected cancer diagnosis in November 2021. He studied English at undergrad and has always been an avid reader, but had never taken the step into writing his own work until after the diagnosis. This is the first short story he's ever written, but he plans on writing more.

Appraisal

by Steve Neal

Mick placed three teeth onto the leathered skin of the crone's outstretched hand. She towered over him, an emaciated giant that stood with a crook in her neck to fit below the ceiling of her cave. She held her palm an inch away from her lone bulbous eye to inspect the offering.

"They're rotten," she tossed the teeth onto the floor beside the scores of other discarded teeth and bones.

"Please, they're fresh," Mick's hands shook at his side.

"Two days."

"I need this."

The crone raised her hand and pointed outside toward the sinuous path that led to her cave. "One day."

Though he walked home through a cool spring night, Mick was drenched with sweat when he made it through his front door. In the hallway, he steeled his nerves and took a deep breath before entering his daughter's room.

She'd already put herself to bed, changed into her

dinosaur pajamas, and nestled beneath her blankets with her stuffed toys.

"Hi sweetie," he said.

"Daddy," she smiled a wide, toothless grin. Three wounds still wept in her mouth. "Can we do a bedtime story?"

"Of course. Remember how I told you about the tooth fairy? Do you want to hear about the thumb fairy?"

Steve Neal is an English-born writer currently surviving the summers of Florida with his supportive wife and less supportive cats. As a lifelong horror fanatic, he enjoys poking at the unknown and seeing what comes crawling out, as long as it isn't spiders.

Snakeslut

by Stephanie Parent

The first time Melanie slept with a man she did not love, she woke with a tiny snake coiled in her hair.

The creature slithered against her neck; she screamed and yanked it with the same force Tim had used to tug her hair last night.

But the thing wouldn't come out. When Melanie attempted to cut the wriggling reptile, her own limbs became impotent. Like last night when Tim's sweaty-slimy body slithered up hers, when his teeth pierced her, snakelike. Injecting venom that left her passive, a Grecian urn existing only to be filled.

Now, Melanie was an empty vessel attached to a miniature monster.

Melanie slept with more men she didn't love. Each time, another snake grew from her head; soon there were so many that she wondered if the men would freeze, horrified. But men saw what they wanted. So she kept going, till she had only enough hair left to wrap around her finger like a wedding ring.

Snakes entwined around Melanie's scalp. Hungry lovers, opening tiny-teethed mouths. And Melanie wondered if a person's own despair could devour them from the inside out.

Her phone rang—Tim. "You still coming?"

"I'm on my way," she answered. "Too late to turn back now."

Stephanie Parent is a graduate of the Master of Professional Writing program at USC. Her short horror fiction has been published by Cemetery Gates Media and Skullgate Media.

Maddalena

by Mo Moshaty

It'll be the death of you, young love, they always say.

She is the center of my universe and my reason for living. As if Mozart himself set the veins, sinew, muscle, and skin into full pulsing vitality graced with love and tenderness and that ruffian smile with a chip in her front tooth.

The white-hot electricity of our bodies as we further intertwined to and fro, in the clandestine alleyways near the river, hexed me with a new passion, Maddalena. I managed to scrape my way into affording Mrs. Benington's boarder house on the river for us. We drank until dawn to our nuptials, and I lay beside a sleeping love I'd never known.

Morning came and my eyes adjusted slowly to the glaze between awake and asleep, and to the round of Maddalena's hip and thigh, the small of her back, the nape of her neck and my arm bare to the bone and bloody in her mouth.

She had eaten me through and licked the bones clean as she worked her way upwards, tossing her head back to open her throat, taking more of me down to the gullet. I wiggled my bones to cradle her head and let love eat me alive.

Mo Moshaty is a genre screenwriter and journalist with Nyx Horror Collective and co-producer of the 13 Minutes of Horror Film Festival featured on The Shudder Channel. With a concentration on psychological and possession horror in her writing, her background as a Trauma Specialist provides a sturdy foundation. Mo is the creator of the course, "Writing Trauma Respectfully for Screen." and was a Guest Lecturer for Prairie View A&M University's Film and TV Program. She has recently partnered with Stowe Story Labs to provide a fellowship for women writers over 40 working in the genre.

Bone Meal
by Caoilfhinn Byrne Hegarty

'Grow through what you go through!' The poster depicts an obscenely peaceful girl with daisies sprouting out of her skull instead of hair. I think of two cats buried in my childhood friend's back-garden, while he solemnly informed me they were full of worms now. The next spring violets pushed out of their little bodies.

My cousin once inhaled a pea, which sprouted in the wet warmth of his lung. He needed an operation. The memory makes me itchy with discomfort. The idea of little seeking shoots anchoring themselves in my brain is worse. I resist retching. Oblivious, my therapist drones on.

Something scratches my nostrils. I scrub impatiently and tug out a green stem with unfurling leaves. Before I can panic, a sharp pain shoots through my right eye and I pull from my tear duct a spine of rosemary. A feathery feeling billows up my throat and I splutter lilies. Roses force themselves out from my ears, bursting the drums with their thorns. I howl. The therapist shifts in her chair, still talking. An unbearable pressure builds in my brain, and I know there are daisies strangling it, just as I know there's ivy all over my ribs, cracking them like old brick walls.

Caoilfhinn Byrne Hegarty was born, raised, and educated in the same ten square kilometers of Dublin, Ireland. She enjoys writing about ugly emotions and the kissing-point between love and hate. As a rule of thumb, if something makes her toes curl, there's a good chance she'll want to pull a story out of it. Her fiction has appeared in the literary journals Caveat Lector and Gluepot.

Privilege
by Jo Bodley

Stuart wore a white suit, a nod to the eponymous Ealing comedy. I was dressed like a New Orleans tart, in a silk peignoir, a feather boa, and my mother's old gold strappy evening sandals. It was a 'Divine Decadence' themed party, and the host, in satin frock coat, britches and powdered wig had proffered me a line of white powder on a hand mirror on the way in, like a demented Mozart.

Without my glasses on I couldn't see anything clearly more than five inches away. Stuart asked me to dance and I noticed at once that he was easily the most attractive man I had ever met.

We left the party early for his flatshare in King's Cross; Stanley Buildings, to be precise.

The bathroom was papered with Manga comics and in the corner was a mannequin wearing a fur bikini.

We explored one another to the sound of Rick James' Superfreak.

'The bath was not draining properly,' Stuart told me later, 'So we called in a plumber. In the waste pipe underneath, he found human teeth!' He laughed.

I did not think it was funny.

Standing on tiptoe I could see, through the bathroom window, prostitutes getting into cars on York Rd.

Jo Bodley grew up in Jane Austen country with four sisters, but there any similarity with 'Pride and Prejudice' in her life and work ends. She has been published in the Croydon Writers' anthology, 'The Trouble with Young Writers,' taken from a quote by Somerset Maughm which concludes, 'is that none of them are under 60.'

Body Image
by Joseph Zak Bailey

"Hi!" the scratch in his thigh flesh spelt out.

He was in the middle of getting ready for work, preparations for the same old slog, when he noticed the mark on his body. Naked, he sat down on his desk chair, his pale, chubby frame exposed. He examined his body. Holding his flab in one hand while feeling the raised scabbed edge with the other. He dug and picked at it, opening the wound. A drop of blood ran down. Falling on the floor. Staining the off-white carpet. It had seen better days but he had long given up on keeping a cleanly home. He sighed and rubbed the mess in with his right foot.

A fresh wound started opening above the previous, as if someone with a needle was writing on his skin.

"Help me," it said.

"Help me?" he read out loud, "How can I help you?"

"End this!" was written on to his stomach.

"End what?"

"Life," formed on his right arm.

"Life?" he echoed.

"End this life," followed on his left arm.

"But who are you?"

There was no answer.

"Are you a ghost?"

Silence.

"A spirit?"

Stillness.

"A poltergeist?"

Nothing.

"Are you Satan?"

Carved into his chest: "No, I am you."

Joseph Zak Bailey is a writer from the south of England. He has previously contributed to fan sites writing about and reviewing television shows, movies and video games. Other people's stories were not enough. He now looks to take over the fiction world where he aims to tackle the bizarrely comedic and comically bizarre.

My Vanishing Bones

by Mark Wheaton

My bones disappear, every day, every day. A toe. A finger. A rib. They've done so since I was old enough to breathe. The pepperer says plague. The priest says devil.

My mother says, "Run."

I do and for miles. My legs wither and my arms recede. I tumble and crawl.

Then I eat an old mousy. It isn't enough, but there is a tickle.

I try a bird. A toad. A pig trotter.

Closer, my diminishing body whispers.

I sever an old lady's leg and gobble it up. Her thigh bone becomes my left thumb. Size, it turns out, matters not. Only bone.

I pulverize a mendicant's skull to replace a vertebra. Gnaw a washerwoman's pelvis until my collarbone re-emerges. Grind a blacksmith's shoulder into a powder I slurp up with soup. I'm rewarded with a re-grown kneecap.

I swallow teeth. Not bones, I learn. Fingernails, neither.

They catch me stealing shins from fresh graves and nail me in a box. They poke my stomach.

"Still bones in there," they say, awed.

Not for long, I want to whisper.

Their nails are through my hands and feet. I lie still as my finger bones dwindle away. The nails loosen. Their skulls will pay the bill.

Mark Wheaton is a screenwriter (FRIDAY THE 13TH, THE MESSENGERS, VOICE FROM THE STONE, etc.) and novelist (QUAKE CITIES, Fr. CHAVEZ trilogy, EMILY ETERNAL, the latter named one of the five Best Science Fiction Novels of 2019 by the Financial Times). His first horror short story, IN THE WATER, appeared in the 2021 Stoker Award-nominated anthology, WORST LAID PLANS, from Grindhouse Press. He has subsequently had stories appear in anthologies from Dark Peninsula Press, Macabre Ladies Publishing, 18th Wall, Sentinel Creatives, Blood Song Books, Hellbound Books, and more.

A Feast of Screams

by Miguel Alfonso Ramos

The last bite is fine as the first, but when I'm done we'll start again.

Immortality is grand—until it isn't.

Rest easy brother, I get as good as I give, it will soon be my time under your thumb's finely honed blades—but for now, I feast.

Who knew the jelly delicacies of your body's inner chambers? The sweet, wet meats and dripping fats? Don't fret or squirm (do squirm). Your sweat flavors my rough tongue.

Witness your raw, shuddering heart, your symphony of hoarse screams, the drumroll of your snapping joints.

Dark winds blow through the cold space. They both shiver without notice.

You'll know truth when I lie to you, so listen while you can. You are my mirror, and even as I wear your skin and shamble shadow-like through your life, this too will end, and you will have your own shattered justice.

I see a glimmer of understanding in your remaining eye. The end, or the beginning, comes. It's a matter of perspective – or rather, of who's feeling the sharp end of the knife.

Let us continue this journey together, following our bloody path towards dark delicacies.

The night falls upon them like a gallows floor, inevitable, sudden.

Miguel Alfonso Ramos lives on the West coast, is a librarian, reads widely and voraciously. He is a musician and has played in several bands, from mariachi to punk rock and bluegrass. He loves to climb mountains, jump into oceans, and ride his motorcycle at night. He writes SF, fantasy, horror and poetry, and is a graduate of the Clarion West Writers Workshop. He is Hispanic, Wyandotte and Chinese, plays chess and D&D, and watches lots of movies. His story "The Cave" was recently published in the anthology "Winter Wonders".

Sizzling Surprise
by Tess P

I tugged my hood tighter to shield the screaming wind. The oversized coat, though not haute couture, hid shabby layers well enough. I glanced at the plastic tub; sparse change insufficient for one coffee.

A red convertible parked, taking two greedy spaces. A stunning piece of shiny kit.

The driver's window slid down revealing a woman, festooned in fur, angrily lighting a cigarette. I thought wearing dead animals had gone out of fashion. She sneered at me, I sighed. Her car, worth the price of a property, yet she threw no coins. My stomach growled.

She flung the door open, tossed the butt at my shoes and for no apparent reason, brutally kicked the perfect paintwork.

What followed next, I could barely believe. The door liquefied, snatched the woman, hurtling her back inside. She screamed as molten metal burned her body, eyes bulging beautifully. Desperate, she sought mine.

I watched her head swing from a broken neck as her flesh flambéed. A delicious BBQ aroma teasingly emitted. My mouth salivated. The boot clicked, tossing a fine tender leg, my way.

I gulped at the gift.

Sadly, the vegan in me could not accept. I thanked the car. It winked one headlamp and shifted away.

Tess is new to both the horror genre and writing shorts. This is her first attempt at combining the two. She has spent the last year penning poetry and in September 2021, self-published "Secret whispers"—a delicious mix of light and dark muses; a collection she had never planned to publish. She tweets micro poetry most days @tess_2020 and is host to #5wordspoet. Tess enjoys supporting creatives, engaging in life chats and light banter within the friendly writing community.

There Are Many Different Kinds of Hunger
by Jolie Toomajan

She floats outside the window glass, bloody mouthed and longing. Her reflection doubles over mine; I am bloody mouthed, too.

Let me in. I'll drink up their bones. Anything for you.

Naked need is a lure. That kind of loneliness sits on the palate, waiting for the tongue to roll past it. Hungry eyes floating in window, bobbing behind my own reflection. I haven't let her in yet. I've wanted to.

This house is made of glass bones. I have replaced so many mirrors already. I know the shatter by location; this was the dining hall. The gilded one. The mirror will be replaced in a few days, ready for the next fight. Let me out.

An invitation is a fragile thing. Not a gift but a decision, like a name. It can't be taken back. The tumbling clicks of broken plaster hitting the floor. Goose down in the air. A broken perfume bottle. Retching and retching and retching. I will never have a sister. Let me be.

My hand brushes against the pane, knuckle first, stroking, descending. The girl outside the attic window rubs her face into the glass like a cat in a kennel, leaving foamy red smears. I let go. Let her in.

Jolie Toomajan is a Ph.D. candidate, writer, editor, and all-around creep. Her dissertation in progress is focused on the women who wrote for Weird Tales and her work has appeared in Black Static, Death in the Mouth, and Upon a Thrice Time (among other places). Despite all of this, her plan for the zombie apocalypse is to pour a bottle of hot sauce over her head.

Mirror, Mirror
by Adam Lippert

On the wall, for the love of God, show me something else. Anything. Except her. The naked old woman stares out from the mirror. She has a saggy belly and wrinkled tits, blood smeared in her grey pubic hair, and glowing red eyes that follow like a Rembrandt portrait. She shouldn't be there. Because I am alone.

I don't know who she is. It doesn't matter. I just want her gone. I hide under the blankets and realize that seeing is better. At least I'd know what she is doing. But I'm too afraid to look.

The nightly nurse must've fallen asleep because they haven't made their rounds in hours.

"Help!"

This room has no windows. No roommate. No belongings. There is only this rock-hard bed and the cheval mirror hanging on the padded wall. And there's nothing I can use to break it. The nurses don't know anything. Why I'm here. How long it's been. Or where the mirror came from.

"Been here since I started," the nurses reply.

I'm sure the woman has answers. Those flickering red eyes are rich with horrible knowledge. She taps on the mirror. The tapping becomes knocking. The knocking becomes pounding. Until the glass will surely shatter.

A. C. Lippert is from Grand Ledge, Michigan and now lives in Lansing. He holds a Master's degree from the University of Louisville and attended his undergraduate studies at Central Michigan University. His fiction has appeared in places like Tales to Terrify, Down in the Dirt Magazine, Loud Zoo, The Meadow, and Conceit Magazine.

Bunker

by Ceres Vega

It was a perfect bunker.

Matthew dug it himself, poured the concrete himself, filled it with supplies himself. It had lights and heaters and ventilation systems powered by generators, a three year supply of food and water, and an excellent kitchen with a dozen ways to turn preserved food into something resembling a decent meal. It even had comfortable beds and a bathtub.

It had his family, albeit his very ungrateful family who really should know better by now. He'd even gone to the trouble of bringing his wife's new husband and son, when he could have said "hell with it" and abandoned them to nuclear fire. His wife and his daughters were all he really needed, but he wanted to be nice.

He even used soft ropes to tie them up before he brought them inside, and had packed soothing lotion in case they rubbed wrong anyway. There was no need to be inhumane about it.

It was only after he sealed himself in, shut down all ways of communicating with the outside world, and untied his family that he realized he'd forgotten to send his men the signal.

How was he going to survive a nuclear attack if he didn't set off the nukes?

Ceres Vega is an aspiring author and actual fanfic writer with a penchant for the strange and unusual. She was born and raised in San Diego, and as a direct result of this she's a subtropical bird with zero winter tolerance and an inordinate fondness for thick, fluffy socks. She also has an inordinate fondness for thick, fluffy cats, and lives with two of them. The rest of her menagerie includes a small and short-furred cat, a crested gecko, and her anxiety demons.

Elixir

by Sara Dobbie

The man across the hall is sleepwalking again. His name is Gavin, but I call him by another name. Through the peephole I watch him travel up and down the corridor, aimless, like a moth. I open the door, hinges creaking, casting a sliver of dim light. I aim to be the flame.

His face resembles a photograph come back to life, a resurrection after countless decades. I've watched him for weeks, spying through my peephole as he comes and goes. Awestruck by the resemblance to a man I once knew, I am finished with waiting. Hidden like a leper inside these four walls, I tell myself his wife will understand. If she knew how it feels to inhabit the endless, empty void, she'd offer me this fleeting chance at redemption.

Of course he offered to help me carry my bags when he saw me struggling, and of course he drank the draft I poured for him. Now he sits in a stupor, as I trace his star sign in a jar of sun-charged water. Immerse my crystal and stir. Lock the door, smooth my silver hair, straighten my withered frame. His eyelids lift and recognition flickers.

"It's you," he says.

"Yes," I answer. "It's me."

Sara Dobbie is a Canadian writer from Southern Ontario. Her work has appeared in many literary journals in print and online. Her magical realism and dark fiction stories have found homes at places like Fiction Kitchen Berlin, Mooky Chick, Twin Pies Lit, and Dreamers Creative Writing. Her debut fiction collection is forthcoming from ELJ Editions in 2022. Her fiction has been nominated for Best of the Net, Best Small Fictions, and the Pushcart Prize. Follow her on Twitter at @sbdobbie.

Mary, Mary

by Laura Fowler

"Mary, Mary quite contrary how does your garden grow..."

I hear their chants each afternoon through my window. Soon one will take the dare. Jeered by the crowd those small feet will come across my boundary.

My gate groans as it opens, a mournful sound, amping up their fear. "Go on" they call, encouraging the brave forward as they stay safe.

Yes, so young, perhaps the youngest yet to try to reach my home. A child in search of adulthood, a show of strength for the others.

Each step firm upon my clover lawn. The vibrations of each movement caressing the roots of my house, feeding us.

They do not yet realise, every step brings them closer to knowing us and forgetting themselves.

With each step a memory taken, a happiness stolen. Their young dreams are so bright and nourishing and the darkness that lies within us craves it.

A knock, a single strike against the door and the running. A dash to the gate and out. Safe, safely away but altered. Changed forever, holes left that can never be filled.

I sit in my room once more and wait, feeling the hunger once more grow, waiting for the chants to begin anew: "Mary, Mary..."

Laura is from King's Lynn, England. She lives with her partner and two sons. She has been writing poems and short stories since she was a child. Her favorite things to do are read, go out on walks with her family, swimming and watching theatre. Her taste in books is eclectic everything from cosy romance to graphic horror but fantasy is her favorite.

Try Smiling
by James Davies

The headlights from oncoming cars grew brighter and
then swept past. They ignored Jack. He held his thumb
out, but he knew nobody would stop. Not on a night
like this.

"Try smiling"

The voice came from very close behind him and
made him jump, made him spin towards it. A man
stood there. He was well dressed, but something was
wrong with his eyes. His pupils were too big, the
whites too small.

"Try smiling. They might pick you up" he said.

When the man spoke, his words seemed to issue
from somewhere other than his mouth, his lips moving
but not matching the sounds he created. The man
stepped closer soundlessly and Jack became
unaccountably terrified. Looking in the man's eyes
was like looking at death. Like something after death.
Something rotten, cursed. Jack tried to speak, but
found he could not.

"Try smiling" the man said, and stepped closer
again. He was inches from Jack's face. Something was
happening to the man's skin. It was undulating like
water, as if it was melting. Jack couldn't move. The

man placed his hands on Jack's shoulders and his mouth contorted into a smile. It grew wider and wider until it was all Jack could see.

James works with computers, but loves to read. He lives in Cheltenham with his wife Kate, and likes to paint, watch films, and enjoys writing short fiction.

Ex

by Josh Holton

Our eyes meet at church. I quickly look away, shame flushing my cheeks.

I wasn't myself when I was with him. He's seen parts of me no one else has, and he knows my secrets. He met my parents. They told him stories and showed him pictures of my childhood.

He's only seen one side of me, but he probably thinks he knows all there is about me. In truth, I only found myself once he'd left. I hope he knows I'm doing just fine without him. I needed him then, but I'm my own person now.

Of course, he didn't leave before he'd had me squirming naked beneath him, trying my best.

I regret the embarrassing, crude things I whispered in his ear, and now here he is, guest preaching the Sunday sermon. I wonder if he discusses me with his friends and colleagues. The things he could tell them…

Maybe he's given me no further consideration. Hopefully he doesn't recognise me. I look totally different now. I can't pretend I've not seen him. I hope he doesn't try and speak to me at the end. I'll leave quickly in the bulk of the crowd, keeping my eyes down.

It's awkward bumping into your exorcist.

Josh Holton is an ex-MMA fighter who took too many blows to the head and now writes and draws the unexpected. He placed in Streetcake's Experimental Writing Prize 2021, Spread the Word's Life Writing Prize 2020, and he was runner up in the Writers' and Artists' Working Class Writers' Prize 2020. Find him on Twitter @JHoltonWriter.

What Men Do

by Cole Brayfield

Our eyes meet among the blood, dirt, and screams. I'm drawn to his mouth and hips.

We dance, our blades like thunder. It's over too quickly when the sweat of my brow, hot and wet, stings my eyes, and his steel slides into me. Sweat drips from the tip of his nose. Then I feel like captured prey, like a deer bleeding, and it hurts. I am ashamed.

I think about him every second the world is dark until a necromancer knocks my bones together. I ignore the sorcerer's commands and walk fast.

When I find him again, the man I saw last, his hair's longer and the lines beneath his eyes deeper. "Who are you?" he asks.

I nearly collapse. I realize I have no face, lips, tongue, no way to say what I want to say, what I'm ashamed to say but wish I could've said long ago. No way to do what I never did, skin meeting skin. No way to cry. No heart or brain or whatever feels loss. He raises his blade. All I have is blade and boney hand. At least we are connected, violent blows, the colliding steel, his muscle, my hollow. At least we connect, over and over.

*Cole has work forthcoming
in Neon and Glassworks and his game Walk with the
Living is available on Steam. Find more from him
at brayfieldwriting.com*

A Snag in the Thread of Reality

by bdyer

Once he got his hands on that thread of ethereal silver, Max decided he would never let it go. He had reached back only moments earlier to tug at something stuck to his sweater but as soon as he touched it, the snag had wormed its way up to his brain, forming new creases of manic hunger and an excited glint in his eyes.

He leaned back, knuckles whitening against the strain as a rip appeared in the middle of nowhere. The hole widened, pouring rays of an unknowable color, staining Max's mind. His mouth let out wailing cackles as a tickle fizzled through his hair, as pustules grew pregnant with blood and puss, as his skin melted and flew down the drain of the universe.

And then the thread pulled back, rewinding the lure from the other side. He only had a second to glimpse a dark reflection heave as his entire body was swept up in the stitching and pulled through unimaginably small spaces, air squeaking out of deflated lungs in a pathetic whistle. He remains there even now, a blubbering scab of flesh in the middle of the air, begging all who pass to kill him. Almost no one goes that way anymore.

bdyer lives in the frozen wasteland of the Northern Midwest where he enjoys going on walks, taking in nature, reading, and watching films of all kinds. A longtime fan of genre fiction, particularly horror and fantasy, he writes as a way of exploring perspectives and explaining the craziness of the world.

Grim

by Verity Holloway

I rise from my den at first dark. The sun sets early in late October, the relics of it cooling under my claws as I commence the Prowl.

It is mine, the Prowl, a liturgy learned by rote. Whether the grass is summer-crisp or at peace under a layer of snow, I make my nightly circuit over tumbled flint and ivy-choked stone.

I greet the Dead with a nudge of my hoary snout. At rest. At rest. At rest.

Intruder.

I smell you. Against the north wall—the place for the unborn, the suicides, for travellers without names—you, Intruder, have made a den. Your sleeping bag is ugly plastic fibre, cold against my tongue.

The sanctuary was built to be open, always. Holy, holy, holy place: locks unthinkable. Then men came, stripped the roof of its lead, tore down the painted screens, trampled the Dead. I howled and raged, unheeded. When the locks came, I slunk to my den to grieve.

Like you.

Between my teeth, your skull is brittle with loneliness. You sigh, sensing me through the wine that dulls your blood.

My tail droops. I am a poor guardian.

I can't keep you warm, Intruder. But I will keep you company.

Verity Holloway is a novelist and history lover living in the East of England. She is the author of Pseudotooth, Beauty Secrets of The Martyrs, and The Mighty Healer. She writes folklore features for Hellebore Zine and her short fiction has appeared in Far Horizons, The Shadow Booth, and The Ghastling. verityholloway.com Twitter: @verity_holloway

Don't Wake the Dead

by Brianna Malotke

The floorboards creaked beneath her feet. As Melody silently moved through the darkness, the daylight trying to sneak its way through the closed shutters, she could feel her heart beating rapidly in her chest. Coming to the end of the long hallway, she could finally see the top of the staircase. She said a silent prayer, hoping to make it to the front door without waking him up. Did Vampires even sleep? The thought drifted through her frantic mind.

She swiftly reached the first floor. The large ornate door was within reach. She took a deep breath and pulled the door open. Sunlight illuminated the entire entry way. After so much time spent in darkness the light was too much, she had to shield her eyes.

But as soon as she reached the grass, everything around her started to dim. The sunlight fading fast as she turned in circles, trying to grasp what was happening.

"Where did you go this time?" his eerie voice bringing her back to reality. She shuddered beneath the icy touch of his hand on her cheek. Those jet-black eyes watching her quizzically as Melody realized she had never left. It was just a dream. She was trapped here with him. Forever.

Brianna Malotke is a member of the HWA. Some of her most recent work can be found online at The Crypt, Witch House Amateur Magazine, Dark Entries Journal, and Sirens Call Publications. Her poems are in the anthologies Beneath, Cosmos, The Deep, and Beautiful Tragedies 2. She has a short story in The Dire Circle, from D&T Publishing. In April 2022, she will have two body horror poems in the Women in Horror Poetry Showcase, Under Her Skin, published by Black Spot Books. In 2023 she will be a "Writer in Residence" at the Chateau d'Orquevaux in France.

Harmony of the Spheres

by R. W. Daniels

Men once hypothesized a Harmony of Spheres. They supposed the ratios between the speeds, positions, etcetera of the planets produced transcendent music. Man bathed in this symphony, but constantly exposed to it, never noticed it. We know this is literally false. Space is a vacuum, containing no fluid through which sound can be transmitted. Still, something like the harmony might be true. Not sound, but background thought, on the periphery of consciousness, ubiquitously experienced but imperceptible.

The harmony became an obsession. I put a plan into motion.

What do you see when you close your eyes? It's not nothing. Your optic nerves still transmit to your brain, you see blackness. To see nothing, you would need to stop the transmission. I needed to cease hearing the harmony of the spheres, so that when I heard it again, I could perceive it. I removed my brain, placed it a neutro-chemical vat. I shielded the vat with lead. No sensory signals from my body. No cosmic rays altering my brain. I didn't even see black.

I spent one week alone.

I can hear it now. It's conscious. A living song. It whispers to me, just like it whispers to you. It is malicious. All it desires is suffering.

R.W. Daniels is a banker who wishes he were anything else. Writing is a familiar escape, but showing that writing to others is less familiar. In addition to writing, R.W. Daniels' time is occupied with baking, tabletop gaming, reading fantasy and philosophy, and planning for the day when he has his first child.

Option 34-Dandelions at the Base of Tyrebagger Hill
by Callum Brampton

Cheaper than anaesthetic and if the literature was to be believed it was also less of a risk. Didn't make it any less intrusive, soon that metal spike would slide into my brain. I would be transported somewhere else whilst doctors performed on my lifeless body. I chose to have option 34 projected into my mind, hills reminded me of home. But as soon as the operation began, I knew something was wrong.

A terrifying reality became apparent to me. The Dandelions looked beautiful, that's what I needed to focus on, I had to imagine how the bench would feel if I was actually resting on it. Anything other than the truth, the damned machine hadn't worked, I was able to see the hills but the rest of my senses were still trapped in reality. Completely powerless as cold metal pressed upon my skin and the searing torrent of pain consumed my mind. I was trapped in a glorified travel brochure whilst my body was subject to sterile steel and the heartless muscle memory of well-paid surgeons.

Months later I still feel absent. I had to leave Scotland. Those hills were no longer home. Even now I crumble at the sight of dandelions growing between cracks.

Callum Brampton started writing late in the pandemic and has begun entering his work into competitions as part of a new year's resolution. He grew up reading Lovecraft's gothic horror and likes to write stories commonly in the genre of dark fiction. These stories focus on how individuals shape and are shaped by traumatic events.

Sacrifice

by Geoffrey Hart

I hesitate at the temple's outer door, breathe deep, then pass within. Only my family's needs matter now.

In the antechamber, the Senior Accountant waits. He takes my badge without meeting my eyes, opens his ledger, records something, then places the badge in a drawer. He closes the ledger firmly. In an ornate glass container on his desk, his testicles float in red ink.

Next, I pass through the chamber of the MBAs, who wait, their eyes gleaming with secret knowledge forbidden to those like me. They anoint my brow with the holy oils that are their order's special purview.

Last, I enter the High Priest's inner sanctum, where final authority vests in those who survived the ruthless culling. I kneel as they taught me, and hold my necktie for the high priestess to take in her elegantly manicured hand. She draws it tight to steal my breath, and holy lust glows in her eyes as she turns to face the High Priest. From his rich robes, he draws the ceremonial knife, which gleams icy white in the cold light.

"We accept your sacrifice," he intones the ritual words, then draws the knife across my throat.

As I fall, my last thoughts are of my family.

Geoff (he/him) works as a scientific editor, specializing in helping scientists who have English as their second language publish their research. He also writes fiction in his spare time, and has sold 46 stories thus far. www.geoff-hart.com

Escape Velocity
by T. K. Howell

Dmitri lived alone in the basin of an impact crater out in the hinterlands. Every night he drove along its rim in his Jeep listening to podcasts about unsolved mysteries and the paranormal. The moonlight illuminated the rim and the woods beyond, but nothing touched the inky soup of the crater. Down below he could see his porch light, a single point, like a lone star in endless space.

Sometimes he saw faces out there in the moonlit woods, floating among the trees. They didn't seem to have any body, they didn't seem to be there at all.

He alternated between clockwise and anticlockwise, fast and slow.

Some nights he trundled at twenty, peering out the window, trying to see if he recognised any of the faces. He waved. They never waved back.

Others nights, he pushed the Jeep all the way up to a hundred, listening to it whine and rattle, wondering if it would fall apart all around him like in the cartoons, wondering if he could reach Escape Velocity if he just drove fast enough

But it didn't matter. Clockwise, anticlockwise. Fast or slow. He never found an off-ramp but the one that led back down into the nothingness and toward his cabin.

T. K. Howell is a writer living on the banks of the Thames. When not writing, he manages ancient oak woodlands and tends to trees that are older than most countries. His writing is often inspired by mythology and folklore.

The Stone Throne

by Neil Parker

He crept closer through the shadows. No air current he noticed. The skeletal remains lay still on the stone throne. Silence. He caught his breath; this was easy he thought. But then no-one had told him the truth. An unnamed horror lay deep within the mountain was the legend. But no-one had seen anything for decades at least.

This should be simple then. A quick scout about, grab any loot, and off without anyone knowing.

He hesitated before the remains. Is that gold? He grabbed at the necklace, pulling at little too vigorously, the gold caressed with surprisingly very little dust. Before he realised there was movement, the remains slid and clattered from the upright.

Carelessly, he thrust the purple cloaked remains off the throne and without realising found himself seated.

A commanding position he mused, before detecting a faint chanting sound. There was no-one else here. Except for the bony legend at his feet that is.

Was this the legend? Not particularly terrifying.

The chanting went on. An ever so slight tremor coursed through the stone work. The remains shifted, creaked, rose.

He had never heard of a lich nor a phylactery. Thoughts drifted as his soul was absorbed into the cold pulsating stone throne.

Neil has spent over 20 years working in the charity sector, in the provision of advice and mental health and homelessness work. Neil has long been a fan of the fantasy and sci-fi genres, playing board games and role-playing games on and off since childhood. Currently writes in spare time, including poetry and creating fantasy campaigns for friends.

Beautiful Boy

by e rathke

She sang for the one within her womb. Hands caressing, she told him she was proud. Gentle, he did not kick or thrash.

Blood on the table, her curses cut through stinking air. Her fury pulled night from the sky, forcing dawn, and labor's stillborn end.

She promised to disembowel anyone who touched her boy. They left her the breathless body.

They demanded burial in holy ground. She said God could go to hell.

That night she cut out his heart, planted it in the backyard, bled herself over him.

She smiled through the funeral, struck the priest when he called the corpse her son.

Each night she bled into him.

A tree of bone grew. She pointed a knife in her husband's face, promised to attend his funeral tearless. He let the bonetree grow. Left.

Months of scarred cultivation, a face appeared. Smiling through tears, she touched him. She cut herself, pressed it to lips, "Drink."

On the day she pulled him from the bonetree, blood clinging to wooden limbs, she cooed, "My beautiful boy."

His clacking feet and hollow voice filled the house. She called her son, fed him blood, listened to his beating heart. "My beautiful boy."

Her boy's bloody mouth smiled, "Mum."

edward rathke lives in Minneapolis. You can read more of his writing at radicaledward.substack.com.

Boned

by Alice Austin

I'll need a complete skeleton for the spell, but you're missing some bones. Not to worry, my love. A few replacements shouldn't matter much. In fact, I can make some improvements.

A monkey's finger for dexterity.

A camel's femur for endurance.

A horse's pelvis for… size.

Ok, I admit it. I'm trying to improve our sex life. Can you blame me? Neither of us were satisfied before and you know it.

I piece you together and begin. Muscle, flesh and skin grow across your new bones. It's good to see you again.

At last, your eyes open.

"Welcome back, my love. Don't be upset…"

"WHAT DID YOU DO?" you scream. Your magic throws me against the wall, and everything goes black.

I wake slowly, aching. My body feels wrong.

"It was an accident," you say. "I'm so sorry. Your

304

neck was broken. I had to bring you back."

"With a few changes," I grumble. "What did you do? A snake's spine for flexibility?"

"And ribs from a rabbit. For your libido."

I'm furious at first, until I realise I'm being hypocritical.

Besides, maybe it's the rabbit talking, but I'm eager to try out these new changes.

"I suppose it's only fair," I say with a smile.

Alice Austin is an author of horror and fantasy – the weirder and creepier the better. She and her partner share their home in Kent, UK with an adorable menace of a cat. Find her on Twitter at @Al_Austin120

Almost There

by K Van Dam

Valentina couldn't stop spitting up her bones, coughing bits of broken, glistening collagen onto murky bathroom tiles.

Ribs were first, of course. Spat out in twos and threes, surprisingly easy considering their curve, like they were eager to eject.

They weren't nearly as alarming as the vertebrae that forced their way, sharp and awkward, up her throat and out from between blue and trembling lips. She'd gotten used to it by the twelfth, like swallowing one of those massive, plastic coated flu capsules in reverse.

The humerus was the worst. She gagged for a solid twenty minutes, trying to work the lengthiest fragment past an oesophagus that didn't want to let it go. It eventually relented, a final retch, and the shattered pieces fell, tinkling into the porcelain sink of the office bathroom, tinting the standing water a pretty, pastel pink.

Her pelvis had to be next. Her hips were TOO WIDE, Lambert had said, sipping coffee with his ill-fitting Hawaiian shirt, his hair unbrushed, his face unpainted, and every single one of his bones allowed to be whole and unbroken.

She smiled at the dim bathroom mirror; the same pink smeared across teeth. She'd show them precisely what they wanted. Only ninety more to go.

K. Van Dam is keeping it goth in wonderfully rainy Washington. She has been published in Cosmos: An Anthology of Dark Microfiction and the Latino Book Review. As a comic writer and illustrator, her work has been published in Puerto Rico Strong and Proud: a LGBTQ+ YA Anthology. She has a BA in Creative Writing from SNHU.

Cornered in the Mausoleum

by John Kiste

The first vampire was a cakewalk; he had bared his breast in defiance to my ash stake. A moment later and he fluttered as hot ashes about the eldritch scene.

The second vampire had just finished hoarding his four potential victims into the vault and was locking it when the third vampire pinioned my arms. My extensive knowledge of Brazilian jiu jitsu served me well now, and I twisted away against his great strength—much to his astonishment.

I grabbed the holy water flask from my deep pocket and shattered it on his startled face. He screamed, shriveled, mewled—and in an instant I had dispatched him with the stake.

The last vampire now realized he was alone. He leapt lithely past me and grasped at my throat, unaware that I had slathered it with garlic. He hissed and I pushed the crucifix from my other pocket into his chest. "Die foul night fiend!" I bellowed and readjusted the stake and lunged. He burst into flames and withered to nothingness.

Now the mausoleum was mercifully quiet. I unlatched the vault and released the four small children. They hugged me close. One of them straightened my calico apron with the deep pockets. "Thank you Grandma," she said.

John Kiste is a horror writer who was the president of the Stark County Visitors' Bureau. He is a double-lung transplantee and organ donation ambassador, a McKinley Museum planetarian and an Edgar Allan Poe impersonator who has been published in Flame Tree Press's Terrifying Ghosts, Third Flatiron, Halloween Horror 3, Mardi Gras Mysteries, Dark Moon Digest, Indomitable Ink, Clockwork Chronicles, A Shadow of Autumn, The Night's End Podcast, The Dark Sire, Jolly Horror Press's Coffin Blossoms anthology, and whose work was included in Camden Press's anthology, Quoth the Raven. You can find him at johnkiste.wordpress.com.

Nyctophobia
by A.R.K. Horton

"They closed the road, Hil," Clive says.

He sounds apologetic, but I don't blame him. He didn't cause the cabin's power to go out or this blizzard. He did plan this impromptu lover's trip, though, and I'd agreed as long as I could bring my nightlight. Now he's in town trying to get a generator and I'm here.

"Hil?"

"I'm here. I just…" I can't continue. Another word and I'll cry.

"You're strong. It's just one night without it."

With only 21% left on my phone, I end the call and rummage around for candles or matches. Nothing, not even dry wood.

I'm twenty-six. I shouldn't need a nightlight.

Distorted memories beckon from my childhood of darkness blanketing me, inhaling me into its gaping mouth. I'd struggled to grasp the bedpost, certain of my death. Yet, somehow, my fumbling fingers found the light switch that night.

I blink away the reflection and stare at my

nightlight sitting lifeless in its socket now. I bundle up and sit with only the phone's glow for companionship. My teeth chatter. My arms tremble. The red sliver at 1% taunts me before it extinguishes.

The rattling darkness greets me with its smothering presence.

I respond with my last "good night."

A.R.K. Horton is a small woman made of round shapes and long sighs. Children and animals surround her in her Florida home. As a pagan witch who grew up obsessed with mythology and folktales, darker stories have always intrigued her. She has published an epic fantasy series called The Telverin Trilogy, and contributed to several anthologies, including the 2nd and 3rd volumes of Skullgate Media's "Tales from the Year Between." You can learn more about her at arkhorton.com.

Forgotten Meal
by Kaylen A. Grimm

Cracking, the door opens to an abandoned condo. Stirred dust floats, the stench of mold and death lingering. The investigator adjusts their mask and reaches for a light with a gloved hand. A lamp flickers before bathing the room in a sickly yellow glow.

Layers of filth covers debris strewn haphazardly on the floor and trinkets on shelves. Two plates and cups rest on a table, black and fuzzy pieces lingering behind. The investigator stifles a gag then moves past the kitchen area, heading to the living room.

Static hums on the TV. Unknown books lay on the coffee table, crooked between the couch and TV. Something lumps on the loveseat, fraying brown hair atop its crown.

Flesh of a corpse melts into cushions, molding to the patchwork fabric. Fine hair scatters around the decaying body, bits of bone visible through dried, torn skin and muscle. Leaning in, the investigator spots a large, deep wound on the victim's neck, old blood staining what's left of their clothes.

Growls rumble in the shadows. The investigator turns, spotting silver eyes down a hallway. Large, yellow teeth glint.

"New food? Finally."

It lunges. Fangs pierce fabric, boring into the investigator's abdomen. Screams echo, not heard by a single soul.

Nestled in the forests of northern Arizona, Kaylen A. Grimm surrounds herself with shelves of books, video games, and manga. In writing, she focuses on darker fantasy, horror, and science-fiction dealing with mortality, morality, and the unknown. When she's not writing, Kaylen's playing video games or watching anime.

The Call

by Katie Young

I dab flour on the screen as I hit 'answer' and tuck my phone under my chin. Wipe my hands on a tea towel.

"Hello?"

There's a pause followed by a sniffling sound.

"Mummy?"

My heart stutters and I sag against the kitchen counter.

"June bug?" It's barely a whisper. I'd named her after the Leighton painting, her thatch of flame red hair reminiscent of the bright orange dress worn by the artist's muse.

"It's me, Mummy."

It's been years but I know my daughter's sing-song voice. That word in her mouth, prelude to her incessant needs and questions. Muh-meee. I'd almost stopped thinking of myself as somebody's mother.

"You can't be..."

My legs buckle. I slide down to sit on the cold tiles. The police never found a body. They'd had various suspects on the hook, tried to make the pieces fit, but eventually the case went cold. Missing, presumed dead.

"I'm coming home, Mummy."

An involuntary, animalistic sound rents my throat. Her father left long ago. He was all I ever wanted, but we couldn't survive his grief.

I crawl to the back door and look out at the patio I buried June beneath.

Some people just aren't cut out to be parents.

"Mummy?"

Katie Young is a writer of dark fiction and poetry. Her work appears in various anthologies including collections by Dark Dispatch, Scott J. Moses, Nyx Publishing, Ghost Orchid Press, and Fox Spirit Books. Her story, Lavender Tea, was selected by Zoe Gilbert for inclusion in the Mechanic Institute Review's Summer Folk Festival 2019. She lives in West London with her partner, an angry cat, and too many books.

Homecoming

by Marissa Snyder

Her first thought when she steered her stuttering car off the interstate toward the hometown she swore she'd never return to was: something isn't right.

She knew this town. Knew it, like she knew the exact number left in her bank account. She'd spent years envying the coal hoppers screaming through, planning her escape.

The diner was replaced by a gas station. The laundromat sign featured an elephant, not a walrus.

As she traversed the streets, the changes multiplied, little details coalescing into a mounting sense of strangeness.

The railway tracks were now a walking path. The cantilever bridge was now cable-stayed.

I was gone three months, she thought.

She read the numbers of her address aloud, to prove she had it right. Because the house was all wrong: white paint instead of blue, arches instead of gables.

And the detail that made sweat bead up on her forehead: the man at the door was not her father.

I'm looking for my parents, she said. But the man seemed confused.

She tried house after house. Each time, no one she knew. No one who knew her.

The cold deepened. The sky darkened. Try one more house, she told herself over and over. Just one more…

Marissa lives in Chicago where she works as a technical writer for an industrial supply company. When she's not writing about pipe fittings and flow valves, she enjoys cooking, watching horror movies with her dog Banjo, and working on her YA fantasy novel. She has degrees in English and Italian literature and is a member of The Chicago Writers Association.

Just Out of Sight
by Alex Sese

Something moves, just out of the corner of my eye. I'm doing laundry, and it shifts at the edge of my sight. It's probably the hamper, fallen by itself. But I turn around and everything is where it should be.

My roommate says I should sleep, that my mind's tricking me. You're just exhausted, he says. So, I lie in bed, and right before I close my eyes, the thing moves just beyond my vision. Like a cat darting between furniture. My roommate was right.

I'm not afraid, just curious. At first. Then it starts feeling closer. Sometimes like a hand reaching out to my elbow.

I'm still tired. Work is demanding and I blame hours of staring at a screen for that thing right at the edge of my sight. It's always too quick, gone by the time I turn around. I think I see something on my screen: a reflection. But by the time I notice, it's gone.

I start to worry, and I tell my roommate. He brushes it off and says I shouldn't seek these things. I don't take his advice, and I wish I had.

I look over my shoulder with a small mirror and see my roommate. He's upside down.

Alex Sese was born and raised in the Philippines and moved to the US at 16. She was disappointed to discover that the weight of all her books was over the luggage weight limit at the airport. She now lives in Morton Grove, IL, with a Kindle full of books and a dream of moving out to the middle of nowhere. When she's not trying to grow tomatoes in her backyard, she's reading science fiction, fantasy, and medical nonfiction.

Fire-Eater
by Chloe Lau

The previous fire-eater of this troop was a fraud. We were short of one act a week before the show, and the boss just picked the first fellow that called in for casting. You should have seen what a fool he made of himself. Sputtering and coughing in the middle of the show. The boss looked right about ready to murder him.

Not long after, the fire-eater guy came down with a fever. When he went to the doctor, the doctor took a look inside his mouth with a flashlight and a wooden ice cream stick. There were clusters of angry red welts blistering at the back of his throat. The ice cream stick came out blackened and smoldering. My tent was beside his—he was screaming the whole night, then it suddenly stopped. I reckon he just left in the middle of the night, because he didn't turn up for breakfast, and the boss refuses to tell us what happened to him. We think that guy didn't know anything about fire-eating at all. He just did it for the pay.

Well, this is your tent. Please don't set anything on fire, especially your own insides. Oh, and breakfast starts at seven. See you around.

Chloe is a seventeen year old Singaporean student that ate pages out of books as a child and narrates the nutritional information on the back of cereal boxes like Shakespearean tragedies as a teenager. These habits have made her a bit of a lunatic, and also gave her a passion for writing poetry and prose of all genres. She has had her works published in her school publication, Chrysalis, for two years in a row.

Serving the Clan
by P.A. Frank

Shadow and flames, moonlight on snow. The clan's chants rose and fell around Risa as she knelt. It had been a hard winter. The bones clicked as they were laid on the plate before her.

Knowing her duty, she swallowed them. She was Clan Shifter, as her mother had been before her and her daughter would be after her. I wonder what I'll be this time. Once she'd been a hawk, tracking an invading enemy clan to their hiding spot. Another time she'd been a boar, seeking out herbs to heal her people of a devastating wasting disease. Always before, she'd been told what type of bones she consumed, so that she knew what shape she would take to serve the clan. But not tonight.

The chanting rose to a fever pitch as she swallowed the last bone and the Shift began. It was painful but quick. The clan fell silent as she peered into a puddle of melted snow to see what she'd become.

A fuzzy brown face with antlers looked back at her. Puzzled, she looked up. Understanding dawned on her as she saw spears pointed at her, firelight glinting off the metal tips. Before she could move, they were plunged into her heart.

P.A. Frank is a modern-day medicine maker turned writer living in the USA. Normal days are spent making things up and writing them down in hopes that people might want to read them, ignoring her cats' wishes to be left alone, and embarking on various land, sea, and sky adventures with her family.

Under Water
by Madeleine McDonald

There is air above me. Concentrate on that. The hands holding me under will release me just in time. I swallow, swallow again, exhale a splinter of air. If I breathe out, I cannot breathe in. No air. My lungs explode with pain.

Concentrate. Think of something else. Cling to the knowledge of air above. Recall poetry once learned by heart. That time may cease and midnight never come. Twenty years ago I read those lines, at university, safe in a foreign land. Only now do I understand that Kit Marlowe, poet, heretic and spy, drunk on words and wine, spoke truth. He knew the true, terrible price that Faustus paid in sealing his bargain with the devil.

My country sold its soul, and there is no escape. Hands grip my hair, tug me upwards. I choke, splutter, gulp air into burning lungs. The man behind the desk stubs out a cigarette, a sign that the interrogation will start again.

He is so young, young enough to be my son. "Where is he?"

How can I answer when I do not know?

He makes a note.

That time may cease and midnight never come.

Midnight has chimed for my beloved country. I stare into soulless eyes.

Madeleine McDonald has published three novels, but prefers the challenge and discipline of short texts. Some of her short pieces have been broadcast on BBC radio, and published in Mslexia, The Journal of Compressed Creative Arts, and other journals.

You Will Know Them by the Lack of Light
by Amy Strong

A streetlight was out in the middle of the block, and a man was standing beneath it. Serai could barely make him out, in the dark. He was staring at her house, and she was staring back, through the front window.

What is he doing there? she thought.

She was used to gunfire, pops and cracks as the neighborhood gentrified.

He's wearing a hoodie, she thought, then immediately corrected herself. Stop.

She leaned back so that she was partially hidden behind a gauzy curtain, semi-veiled, like a buried bride. And then he reached behind him, as if reaching for his wallet. And then he pulled out a machete.

Oh, shit.

He slapped the blade against his palm and took a decisive step off the sidewalk. Serai bolted up the stairs, scurried on shaking legs into the bedroom. No phone in her pocket. No landline. Is the front door even locked? Ask Alexa for help—yes, that's it!

"Alexa, call the police!"

"What is it you want me to do?"

"Alexa," Serai hissed, "Call the police."

"Cull the thieves," Alexa replied. "The day when registered Democrats will be slaughtered in their homes. The signal is: you will know them by the lack of light. Was that helpful?"

Amy Strong is a classical flutist and former attorney now working as a freelance writer in Chicago.

No Such Thing as a Guilt-Free Lunch

by Caitriona Spratt

The dripping in the frigid cave never ceased. With her pale, bony fingers she reached up and stroked the edge of a stalactite. She could feel the calcium working its way through her skin, entering her vessels, and finally resting on her bones. She calmly lowered her head and gazed longingly at his bones. Bits of flesh still rested upon them. It took a few days before they would begin to dissolve into the luminous streams that crept along the cave floor.

Her right shoulder twitched twice before she circled the skeleton for a final time. The walls of the cave allowed her to stay upright. She believed that there was a time when she could walk by herself. Run without by herself. Times that had long since vanished. She missed the way the man had looked at her. She missed the colour of his eyes. She had forgotten what it was to be alone. She wished she had not eaten him.

A loud creak signified the opening of the stone

entryway above her head. A squirming creature was lowered down. It was a man. His eyes opened wide with terror as he took in what lay before him. This man's eyes were hazel, she observed.

Caitriona Spratt is a twenty-one-year-old from Dublin, Ireland. She is in her final year as a student of single honours history. She has loved creative writing as a past-time since she first started writing stories as a young girl. In her spare time, she enjoys reading, going for walks in nature, travelling, and exploring old bookshops.

Red light /Green Light

by Debbie Iancu-Haddad

The baby is screaming.

"Sush, sweetie, sush." He won't sush. Kicking his little legs he bellows his discomfort for all to hear. Panic assaults me as I can't calm him down. My fear envelops us both in tension so thick I can barely shuffle forward.

"MOVE FORWARD," a disembodied voice orders.

Harsh lights reflect off metal surfaces. The cold freezes me to the bone.

I can't move. My feet have stuck to the floor. They know what happens when we reach the front.

The woman behind me places a hand on my back, a gentle pressure between the shoulder blades, propelling me onward.

"The sooner you do it, the sooner you can leave," she whispers.

I nod, accepting her advice. We're both helpless participants in the unbearable ritual prescribed by our rulers.

I'm almost at the front. Long lines of women stretch out on either side of me. The machines are faceless.

I feel the same, no face, no name, clutching my baby to my breast.

He stares up at me, complete trust in his beautiful eyes.

"PLACE OFFSPRING IN THE RECEPTACLE," the voice orders and I comply.

The light turns green, "APPROVED."

I grab him.

Beside me a mother wails as the lights turn red.

Debbie is the author of "Speechless in AchtenTan" coming Feb 22 from Skullgate Media (YA SFF).

Her hobbies include participating in anthologies (seven to date), writing vss on Twitter and buying way too much stuff on Aliexpress. Her day job consists of giving lectures on how to use humor and serving as a chauffeur for my her two teenagers. Residing in Meitar, Israel. Follow @debbieiancu

www.debbieiancu.com

The Pitcher

by Sam Lesek

The scent that wafted through the cavern's tunnels was earthy and sweet, like an overripe fruit. He readjusted his headlamp and wiped the sweat from his brow with his wrist.

He had explored similar caves in the past, but this one felt the most labyrinthine--its chthonic corridors ran deep enough into the earth to make each footstep feel like a step towards something forbidden.

He continued trekking through the dark. The salivating scent urging him deeper despite the narrowing tunnels pressing against his body.

The stagnant sweetness led him down a steep descent. Stone taking on a brighter appearance--verdant and punctuated with a fleshy red--as he lowered himself into the pit. The cavern's cragginess smoothened, becoming waxy under his callused fingertips.

There was a splash, and then the sensation of cool droplets landing on his face. He shined his headlamp around the pool, ripples radiating from around his calves.

There was a slight tingling where a droplet had landed. Gripping the pit's waxy walls, he tried pulling himself up only to slide back into the pool.

Spots on his face started to sear. He dug his nails into the pitcher's cup in another attempt to escape, but she refused to let him go.

Sam Lesek is a writer of speculative fiction and poetry from Toronto, Canada. Her work has appeared in Night Terrors Vol 5. and Chlorophobia: An Eco-Horror Anthology, and is forthcoming in Monstroddities by Sliced Up Press. Find her on Twitter @SamLesek

This Old, Old House

by Sarah Matthews

It's probably nothing to worry about.

Old houses make noises all the time. Creaks, groans, growling voices whispering your darkest sins…

With this kind of plaster, you're gonna see a bit of bleeding. If it starts dripping from the ceiling, just set a bucket under it. Don't bother trying to clean it up unless you have a shitload of holy water on hand.

Speaking of holy water, don't try that on the thing in the hall. It only makes the thing angry. Sage won't work, either. Best to ignore it and avoid its oozing tendrils. They tend to burn if they touch you.

The toilet is gonna gurgle and chuckle wickedly. It's got Cthulhu in it. Yeah, that Cthulhu. Pour some drain cleaner down there once a month or so—that usually keeps it at bay. You could get a new toilet but finding a plumber who'll come out this far in a wood where demons caper and gibber behind every tree is going to be expensive.

Lucretia's the eyeless girl who crawls backwards

up the stairs. Her birthday's this Friday. Don't forget it, or she's apt to steal your soul.

But a little mold? Nothing to worry about. Even if it does have human teeth.

Sarah Matthews is an author from Southern Indiana. Her work has been published in anthologies from Eerie River Publishing and Black Hare Press. She also has published her own collection of short stories, Jubilation Grove and Other Nightmares. Follow her on Twitter @superbfinch.

Night Folks

by Robin Wallington

They come only after the sun sets, when the forest edge is half submerged in marsh mists and the wetland chorused with frogs. In the quarter moon's light, mosquitoes hover like helicopters invading a foreign land and a vixen howls and slips away as if through a portal to her earth where she'll eat her own young in terror.

Dark trees like staves aid their approach as they slide from shadow to shadow to reach the curtained window which inches ghost-like in a non-existent breeze.

As I fight oncoming sleep, they rise as liquid columns to stand in the corner beside the wardrobe, forming two piles of bones like the regurgitated remains of the wooded owl who turns his face away, alarmed into silence.

They turn their damp gourd heads with hollow eyes, lit within by fireflies and mouths sewn shut; pale arms lined and cut, all dressed in rags and holding still like heron seeking fish to spear at my heart and snatch the silver life within.

I bite my lip to stay awake and stare, for when I no longer see them, it's time for fear.

Outside, on the back veranda, my knowing parents slug pale, golden shots and pretend the world is bright.

Robin Wallington writes fiction and poetry from his home in the fantastically literary city of Oxford, UK. For the past 4 years he has run the Creative Writing Group at Oxford University Press. He hasn't been published, and he's not won any awards, but he's OK about that, he writes for the simple pleasure of it.

The Earth Offers Sacrifice to the Sanguine Sky

by Rob D. Smith

Carl thought there must be fifty turkey vultures soaring in the red Spencer County sky as they drove the windy Breashears Road. Kelly thought there might be a hundred. They both agreed there must be a bloated and stinking deer carcass nearby. Every buzzard in the Bluegrass state would be circling soon. Blot out the sun.

Around the bend, Carl slowed their car to a stop. An untold number of vultures were on the asphalt road crowding a dead deer. Kelly told him to roll up the windows. At first, he thought it was because of the putrid scent of decay, but a glance at her made him realize the buzzards spooked her. Can't we go around them?

He inched the nose of the car around the deer and some of the vultures moved. He tapped the horn. That rattled a vulture feeding on the deer. It cast his blue eyes at them. A boy wearing a cloak of oily black feathers. He hopped backward and screeched. Deer fat and gore smeared on his cheeks and cracked black lips. The boy crawled on the back of the largest vulture and it unfurled massive wings. Flapping until it carried the buzzard boy into the cloudless hungry sky.

Rob D. Smith is a common man attempting to write uncommon fiction in Louisville, KY. His work has appeared in Apex Magazine, Shotgun Honey, The Arcanist, Thriller Magazine, Bristol Noir, Rock and a Hard Place Magazine, Tough, and several other crime, horror, and speculative anthologies and online magazines. Follow him on Twitter @RobSmith3

An Unholy Communion

by Hank Helstrom

This happened.

My mother was nine-years-old when, before school one day, she and two friends stopped in at their local church. The place empty, they spread out, genuflected, entered their respective pews and knelt to pray.

They each sensed something amiss. Suddenly, a black baseball-sized orb materialised in the nave. Roughly three feet above ground, it flew down the aisle on a flat trajectory. Just before reaching the altar, it vanished, accompanied by a loud *thwack*, as if striking concrete. A second orb then appeared at the original starting point, again flew, and again disappeared just shy of the altar with a *thwack*.

This cycle continued, the girls eventually looking to one another for clarification and, futilely, for help. They found only fear.

Suddenly sensing a new presence, my mother looked down to find two imprints forming on the cushioned kneeler next to her, as if someone had joined her in prayer.

The girls catapulted out of the church's main entrance, their muffled cries graduating into piercing screams.

Sixty years later, they all remember that event the exact same way. Though they never acquired an explanation, they agree on two things:

    1. Some entity exists beyond our dimension.

    2. It is dark and malicious in nature.

An American refugee, Hank Helstrom is currently seeking asylum in Ireland, the land of his ancestors. An overworked tech employee, he aspires to be...anything else. After reading a Stephen Graham Jones book, Helstrom now fancies himself as a future hotshot horror writer. Here goes nothin.'

Strained Faces

by Adam Smith

Eve smiled more than most goths from their small town; meaning she smiled more than her dad. It was a habit she had tried to break, desperate to present as she saw herself.

She stared at the homemade talisman in her hand and said, "I think it's right."

Headlights from Maybelline's Nova washed over the two, sent their thin shadows to climb the pecan tree that stood off the park's sidewalk. Maybelline's hand cupped Eve's, the talisman's edges sharp against their skin. She said, "You did a really good job."

"I just used photos I found on the internet."

They walked, hand in hand, to the tree's roots. They rested on their knees, dug a small hole in the dirt. "Now we just bury it and say the words," Eve said.

They pressed their foreheads together and whispered to any forces within spellshot.

Felled pecans split open, the sound of yellow rang through their hearts.

Maybelline opened her eyes first. A small thing; bat wings and a duck's bill, a fat stomach with twigs for legs that sat over the hole. Its teeth glared through the wet slime and shone purple. "Hey lovely," she said.

Eve didn't strain against her smile. They had done it. Together.

Adam Smith has written traditionally in comix. His first book, Long Walk to Valhalla was nominated for an Eisner & Harvey award in 2016. He contributed to the Gem nominated Jim Henson's Labyrinth: Shortcuts, was featured in D.C.'s New Talent Showcase, wrote the comix sequel to Dark Crystal, Jim Henson's Beneath the Dark Crystal and several other creator owned stories including, The Down River People, chosen as one of New York Public Library's 50 Must Read Comics. He is slowly and clumsily working his way into prose. You can find him not saying much on Twitter @ASmithWrites

Off the Beaten Path

by Jeanne E. Bush

He hadn't meant to open the door, but it was simply laying there on the ground, deep in the woods.

The day was clear and warm, beautiful in the late fall. As he hiked along the narrow trail, breathing in the piney scent of the evergreens, listening to the birds calling, and hearing the wind rustling through the boughs above, he felt a growing sense of uneasiness.

Something caught his attention off the trail, a reflection through the trees. He paused, then carefully moved off the path, snaking among the trees to find out what had distracted him from his hike.

He came upon the door suddenly. In fact, he almost stepped on it, blending with the ground. The dark wood gleamed softly, and the bright silver doorknob glinted in the streaming sunlight. He looked at it for a moment, then he couldn't resist. Cautiously, he reached down to turn the knob and pull.

The first demon from the underworld ate him whole, bones crunching. Then hundreds of others emerged from the door triumphant and joyful, running into the world to create their havoc and chaos. When the mayhem had calmed, the woods became silent once more, and the door slammed closed. Until the next time.

Jeanne E. Bush has published non-fiction articles in several Oregon newspapers and served as a marketing and research analyst for Oregon State University's quarterly magazine, Oregon's Agricultural Progress. She has also done freelance copy- and layout-editing for Sterling/Chapelle Publishing. Her first horror story, Wheels, is scheduled to be published later this year in the anthology "Chromophobia" (Strangehouse Books/Rooster Republic Press). She currently lives in Oregon with her husband, Bill.

Reflection

by Julia LaFond

My reflection came home late.

"Where have you been?" I grumbled at the mirror. She gave no response aside from a smirk as she settled into place.

We reached for the washcloth in unison as I wiped off my makeup. If only I could wipe away my exhaustion so easily. Or my lingering sense of unease.

When my reflection first disappeared three weeks ago, I panicked. Summoned by my screams, so did Dave – he, too, saw nothing but empty glass in the mirror. We were still trying to figure out what to do when my reflection sauntered back. Once we realized I wasn't a vampire, we calmed down. After all, what were we supposed to do about a wandering reflection?

Morning came. Dreading another day at the office, all I wanted was to stay in bed with Dave. But I dragged myself to the bathroom to prepare for another day of spreadsheets and Blaire's catty insults.

My phone rang.

"You don't need to come in today," my manager informed me shakily. "There's been… an incident. The police said not to tell anyone, but –"

I switched on the light, and my heart dropped into my stomach.

"Blaire's dead."

My grinning reflection wiped blood from her face.

Julia LaFond is a geoscience/astrobiology PhD candidate at Penn State, where she regularly attended the Creative Writing Club pre-pandemic. Her horror comedy poem "The Dullahan" was recently featured in the short story dispensers hosted in a collaboration between Short Edition and the Penn State library system.

The Crabs

by Felix Bartel

On a secluded beach a man lies unmoving. He is not bound, but has been injected with a nerve agent. The toxin relaxes his muscles but does not numb him. His captors wanted him to feel his fate.

There is a stir in the sand. Then he is prodded, gently at first, by needle-like limbs. The man manages to twitch and the limbs retreat but they soon return. With greater confidence. Greater force.

A screeching gurgle pierces the night. The man's head rolls in the direction of the sound. His gaze is met with hundreds of black eyes, glimmering in the moonlight. They are expressionless. Thoughtless. Pitiless.

With jerking movements like puppets on strings the crabs advance. The man tries to call for help but can only flap his mouth like a beached fish. His writhing tongue must look like a worm, for here the crabs attack first. Before he can close his mouth, thick claws prise it open. He can only watch as pincers rip and tear, feeding chunks of flesh into twitching, churning mandibles. The man coughs and spits, trying not to choke on his own blood. Black eyes glimmer. Blood sprays. Sharp limbs tear the sand as they advance. The night is young.

Felix Bartel is an aspiring writer from Sweden. He enjoys mixing cocktails, crafting sentences and getting help with writing bios.

Never Lessens
by Richard Barr

Spastic, painful convulsions contracts the gut and tightens the airways. Mass Formation Psychosis is denied but all who are afflicted bug out and mallet one another in the ruins of the old Sainsbury's. They mash each other's skulls with ferocity and fierce indifference.

Behind banks of glaring CCTV monitors, empty chairs and mugs of coffee long gone cold are sniffed by rats. They nibble around the blue mould emerging from the crusts of hastily put together sandwiches left untouched in the gloam of the unobserved monitors, a patchwork of wide, bright streets and inky, shadowy alleys.

Regularly, shrieks echo down the halls of asbestos choked tenements. Wild, banshee howling issuing from confused and desperate girl-mothers, who bring themselves to drown their slimy new wains in slop buckets; smother them with rags doused in turps; kick them to death or leave them out for wild cats to devour.

The day-to-day will appear as a mountain to be climbed. An assailant to best. Burning towers will stretch to a far horizon, while what circles between them are carrion birds, dark flocks clouding the low hanging skies, circling eternally and always eating off a feast of the perished, which never lessens.

At night, the howlings of the girl-mothers cease.

Richard Barr's had several stories published in the last few years, including in Lancaster University's The Luminary and The Big Issue. More recently he's been published in The Honest Ulsterman, New Critique, Sonder Magazine, Misery Tourism and Bristol Noir. Stories this year have featured in Terror House Magazine and Punk Noir, with work upcoming in Janus Literary and Apocalypse Confidential.

They Walk

by Charlie Carr

The sun goes down, and they begin to wake.

They crawl out of the undergrowth, into the cool air.

They don't look up, don't admire the stars.

They can't see them. They can't hear the leaves crunch beneath their feet. Can't smell the trees that surround them.

All they can do is walk.

And search.

They wander the countryside trying to find It. That which was stolen from them.

They walk until the sun comes up, and then, they relinquish themself to the ground. The soil swallows them, keeps them safe until the day's end, then spits them out so they can continue their journey.

Eventually, they reach a house. Inside they could find It. They press their wet face against the glass and peer in. It's then that they see it, a sleeping form, shrouded beneath a blanket. Could that be It? That which is rightfully there's? Can they finally take It?

They press at the window, trying to get through,

but to no avail.

They walk around to the front of the house. They try the door; it's locked. Reluctantly, they move on.

It doesn't matter. They'll find another one.

But until then, they walk.

All of them.

Every night.

Searching for their skin.

Charlie Carr loves to read classic literature, especially novels of a gothic nature. They like to write stories that follow a horror or sci-fi theme that have an ambiguous tone. They only started writing in the last couple of years and have had a short story published in Glittery Literary Volume 4.

Uncle Unwin's Urn

by Tim O'Neal

Mom kept Uncle Unwin's urn in the back cabinet, where she'd never have to see it.

"Thank God, he's dead," she said.

"Why's that?"

She exhaled a moms-only sigh. "He was a conman, Nolan. He'd cheat a corpse out of its casket. And laugh."

"Can I see his ashes?"

"NO!" she said.

"Why not?"

Her eyes hardened. "You've heard of Pandora's Box?"

I nodded.

"That's why. Nothing good will ever emerge from Unwin's urn. Promise you won't?"

I agreed, but once she stepped out, I pulled down the vase. Something rattled inside. I removed the top, but didn't find the ashes and bone chips I'd expected. Instead, a mummified miniature Uncle Unwin stood there, blinking in the light.

He grinned. "Heeeyyy, kiddo."

"Um."

"Lemme out for just a second, huh? No one's gotta know."

I'd never met a mini talking mummy, so I obeyed, pinching him onto my palm.

"Thanks, kiddo."

His slippery smile spread and rapidly became an expanding black hole. It swallowed his skull, my hand; I tumbled into the viscous darkness.

When I woke, I realized *I* was trapped inside the urn. In the back cabinet where no one would ever look. And Uncle Unwin had vanished.

Tim has sold 11 previous short horror and dark fiction stories. His tale "The Face Thieves" won first place in Page Turner Magazine's writing contest. His work has appeared in publications including: D&T Press, Red Cape Publishing, and the Canadian FrostZone Zine. He lives in Colorado.

Blink

by Dario Reed

I used to think that when I blinked, I broke the speed of light. My vision faded for a millisecond, so I thought *my eyelids moved quicker than light*.

I think of this now as the glue binds my eyelids to just below my eyebrows.

I've tried tape, piercings, blue-tack, and even sheer terror to keep them open. There are times when I want to give up, when I shut my eyes for a second, but my bedroom door shakes and the heaviest footsteps sound in the corridor outside that I spring them back open immediately.

Hayley told me it was harmless, that college kids do it all the time. It was on her list-of-quintessential-college-experiences.

When the wooden block moved under my fingers though, moving letter to letter, I wanted to run away.

I couldn't.

I couldn't look away.

I couldn't close my eyes.

Now I never can.

I use one of those blindfolds to sleep at night, but I

can *feel* it. The warm breath from that wet snout. The 12-inch tongue lolling to one side. Matted fur, vertebrae pushing out its back. Its large eyes an inch from mine, nothing but flimsy fabric between myself and *that demon* who will never let me blink.

Dario has been an avid reader of coming-of-age and science fiction novels, in particular books by John Green and Andy Weir; his favourite book is The Martian. Dario primarily writes screenplays, but has expanded into short fiction after reading King's "On Writing", which also inspired him to read more horror novels. Dario hopes to take his writing further, both in short fiction and long-form screenwriting.

Fever Pitch

by Jen Mierisch

She shouldn't have pissed off a professional softball player.

I practiced at Frazier Park, where a tree had a knot five feet high. In the creek, I found a smooth rock, just the right size.

It took practice to master the overhand throw. I savored the satisfying *thud* each time the rock smacked the knot. The tree bark was the color of her hair, minus the tacky highlights.

Learning the date of the rehearsal was easy. She never shut up about the wedding plans, tagging him in every post. He'd never unfriended me, his forgotten castoff.

In the empty balcony, facing the altar, I stretched my triceps. Right on schedule, the church doors swung open below. Their laughter echoed as they strolled between the pews, his arm draped around her skinny shoulders. I gripped the stone with gloved fingers.

For a second, I hesitated. Did she really deserve this?

Pivoting, I hurled the rock with all my strength, catching myself against the railing just as the rock sliced the bald spot on the top of his head.

To the soundtrack of their screams, I sprinted down the stairs and out the side door. If this ended my career, so what? I had pitched a perfect game.

Jen Mierisch's dream job is to write Twilight Zone episodes, but until then, she's a website administrator by day and a writer of odd stories by night. Jen's work can be found in Horla, Dark Moments, Sanitarium, and numerous anthologies. Jen can be found haunting her local library near Chicago, USA. Read more at www.jenmierisch.com.

Double Death

by J.J. Munro

His sun went down when yet 'twas day

Death snatched him suddenly away.

I tore my gaze from my weathered tombstone. I didn't want to read the rest of that doggerel. I was George Pickett, and I didn't doubt that a few of my burnt bones were still down there somewhere. As for myself, I had stepped back from the Afterlife in search of justice.

Emmanuel Pickett, my treacherous younger brother and author of my epitaph, had set my house alight. That was 83 years ago, and he had prospered from my agonising death in the flames. He even claimed my widow for himself!

But now, as I crossed the cemetery to his grave, I steeled my hollow vaporous form to make him pay. I would scatter his wretched bones to the four winds so he could never find peace/

I breathed on the stone slab covering his pit and watched it crack open. Holding my hands over the earth beneath, I caused it to shift aside until at last, his wooden coffin came into view.

"Emmanuel," I whispered, "come out."

And he did, the wood exploding in splinters, his

skeleton leaping up, holding a blazing torch that enveloped me with fire for the second time.

James Aitchison is an Australian author and poet. As J. J. Munro, his work has appeared via Akashic Books and Horror Tree.

Dunno

by R. G. Hewitt

It's a hell of a job. I'm knackered and so's my mate Ron. We're a team see, I'd never be able to cope on my own. The boss is so bloody particular, got be done just so and he's walking about and you can't be sure 'e ain't watching.

Putting the posts in can be a bitch. You got dig deep, drop the pole in and ram the earth down hard. And you gotta get 'em going straight up, exactly vertical, know what I mean? If you don't then when they takes the weight they can fall over and you don't want that 'cause that would upset the boss and you definitely don't want to upset Vlad. No way.

Getting them up there is a real bastard. I mean, they don't want to go, obviously, so they don't exactly cooperate. So me and Ron have to wrestle the buggers up to the top with them all naked and slippery and shouting and screaming.

Then positioning their assholes over the sharpened end takes some doing but once we drop 'em on gravity takes over. We sometimes have to push a bit until the point comes out their mouths. Hell of a days work and the pay's rubbish.

Enjoying a life-long fascination for the human psyche as well as stories and poetry, gestalt therapist R.G. Hewitt has succumbed to the irresistible passion of writing. It's in the writing that he finds himself in ways that even psychotherapy isn't able to. His first books have been published and despite fitting in the elderly category, he has only just started.

We Aren't Supposed to Talk About What Happened to Libby

by Chrissie Rohrman

I used to love the ocean. Not anymore. Not after what happened to Libby.

"Bet you're too chicken-shit to jump."

Echoes of Heidi's dare follow me everywhere, but it's Libby's shriek as she was dragged toward the cliff's edge that haunts my dreams.

"I can't swim!"

Either Heidi didn't believe her, or just didn't care.

A familiar laugh rings out from the end of the hall. I duck toward my open locker, unable to face her. My hair lifts as Heidi stalks past, a breeze of her own making. In her wake, a whiff of salty sea air.

Libby thought we wanted to be friends.

For a moment, I'm back there, gaping down at the foaming sea, the spot where Libby's head disappeared into the depths.

My arm aches where Heidi grabbed me.

"We weren't here," she hissed. "Not a word about

this, to anyone."

My gaze drops to the dingy linoleum. I open my mouth, snap it shut, turn to walk in the opposite direction. When the screaming starts, I act as surprised as everyone else.

Maybe I should have warned Heidi about the line of damp footprints trailing after her.

But she's the one who said not to talk about what happened to Libby.

Chrissie Rohrman is a Training Supervisor who lives with her husband and herd of fur babies in Indianapolis, Indiana. An addict of writing competitions, her short stories have been published in various online and print magazines. She is currently drafting the first book of a fantasy trilogy.

Merchandise

by Lauren Scharhag

Word has a way of travelling in occult circles. Certain items had started to turn up on the market: a vial of blood here, a feather there, even an eyelash. All said to be possessed of extraordinary properties. Relics typically come from the dead, but alive or dead, I had to see for myself.

I tracked down the supplier, operating out of a little nowhere town near Jacksonville. I followed him to his house, staked it out for a few days.

Out back was an old barn spray-painted with what, to the untrained eye, might look like graffiti, but I recognized as the infernal alphabet. Inside was an old dog pen with a creature hunched in the corner. It was so still, so covered in filth and matted feathers, I thought it must be dead. Still, I banished the dark wards surrounding the building and used bolt cutters to break the locks. As I stepped inside, the creature stirred, chains clinking as it shifted.

Its skin took on a faint glow. When it raised its head, I saw that not even the ravages of abuse could mar its beauty.

"Are you here to save me?" the angel whispered.

I laughed. "Sorry, pal, but I'm the competition."

Lauren Scharhag is an associate editor for GLEAM: Journal of the Cadralor, and the author of thirteen books, including Our Miss Engel and The Order of the Four Sons series (with Coyote Kishpaugh). Her work has appeared in over 150 literary venues around the world. She is the recipient of multiple awards, including the Seamus Burns Creative Writing Prize and a fellowship from Rockhurst University for fiction. Her work has also been nominated for multiple Best of the Net and the Pushcart Prizes. She lives in Kansas City, MO. www.laurenscharhag.blogspot.com

Waning Crescent

by Miranda Maples

I step back from him, he's squirming and gurgling, his throat slit. I watch and wipe the blood from the blade on my bridal trousseau, remembering my mother's words the day before.

Go down to the sea. This spring weather is a harbinger of omens but also of fortunes. Your youth is the best currency, and too soon it will be gone. It will be a memory to give you comfort in the cold nights, in the darkness when he comes to you. When you are writhing in pain giving birth, your insides wrenched open. When your hands are bleeding from being chapped by the cruel winds coming over the ragged cliffs, the freezing salt spray stinging your eyes. You can remember the spring in the darkest of winters, like a balsam for your soul. It's the best we have right now. Mayhap you find solace.

Naked, I go to the sea. I know the tales of the creatures who come from the deep to wayward young women. My mother's words again, "You were born under a dark balsamic moon, but from this dark womb you have power; the night waters are your home."

Finally, I hear them call, and I answer back with ancient words.

Miranda has always loved writing, especially horror and dark fiction, and she has just started down the uncertain and scary path of trying to become a published (and paid) writer. Miranda grew up in a very small, very rural town in the Appalachian mountains. After working a full-time graveyard shift at a hospital while attending college, she finally got her Bachelor of Arts in English from The University of Tennessee. Miranda loves baking, reading, writing, yoga, the ocean at night, going to the movies alone, and nerds-out on all things spooky and weird.

With M'Alice

by Jane Bidder

Daisy stomps down the cellar steps, bristling with the righteous indignation of a seven-year-old unfairly scolded. Hating Tommy for his crocodile tears. Hating Mum for taking his side.

Mum's forbidden her to come down here, doesn't want her playing with "that mountain of old junk" left by their home's former owner. But Mum's "junk" is Daisy's "treasure", the cellar an Aladdin's cave, luring her with its siren call.

A shaft of light from the high window points to a mouldering box. Daisy reaches for it. Fumbles. It teeters, falls, spewing out its innards. An age-blackened silver casket bursts open as it hits the floor.

A flash.

An apparition, exotic as a fairy tale.

Daisy gasps. 'A lady genie. Cool!'

'I am M'Alice.' The silvery voice is musical, enchanting. 'I can grant one wish. Choose wisely. If you choose at all.'

'Of course I'll wish.' Affronted. 'I wish Mum would never tell me off again.'

A smile crawls over M'Alice's lips as she vanishes.

Screaming.

Tommy's screaming.

Daisy pelts upstairs. He's in the kitchen with Mum. Now Daisy starts screaming too.

Mum is whimpering. Eyes wide, bulging. Fingers clawing her face where her mouth should be.

Mum will never tell Daisy off again. Her mouth has disappeared.

Jane Bidder lives in the South-West of England. Her stories have been published in Secret Attic and Glittery Literary anthologies. Jane first took up the pen during lockdown to exercise her little grey cells. She is frequently aghast at what flows forth.

Bureau of Special Services Report Concerning an Uncovered Skeleton
by T. T. Madden

<u>Subject Designation:</u> C-52

<u>Description:</u> One (1) humanoid skeleton of a radically altered structure, bearing a total of six (6) arms, two (2) digitigrade legs, and vestigial tail. Spine elongated to accommodate for extra limbs. Skull bears a small set of antlers, snout, and set of mandibles in place of lower jaw. Height and armspan each totaling eight feet. Confirmed skeleton is not composed of bone, but exact material is unknown.

<u>Origin:</u>

Discovered in the basement of an ancient cathedral in the woods of the European city of Wisborg. It was confined within an ornate oak coffin or sarcophagus. The coffin was sealed with rusted chains and covered in unknown, intricately-carved symbols (see attached photographs for additional reference). Only one word was intelligible, carved on the inside of the coffin itself; Kujara.

Additional Notes:

Causes a harsh illness in those who look upon it for
any extended period of time. Symptoms include
confusion, dizziness, vomiting, and fainting. A Bureau
artist attempting a restoration was only able to avoid
becoming violently ill by observing for intervals of a
maximum of three minutes and thirty-three seconds.

Further Action:

Requires additional testing to determine its
composition, origin, and etymology of the name
Kujara, as well as any possible practical applications.

*T.T. Madden is a nonbinary, mixed-race writer from
Baltimore, and recent nominee for the Pushcart Prize.
Their work has appeared in Ligeia Magazine,
Alternating Current, and Lamplight, among others.
They have work forthcoming as part of the Nighty
Night with Rabia Chaudry podcast, and currently
work as a showrunner for Hunt A Killer.*

Twitter @ttmaddenwrites.

Madeleine

by Barry Hale

Madeleine waits. Outside, the Paris pavements bake under late August sun, but deep in the Metro the air remains cool. And Madeleine waits, as she waits every day, for the moment when he will arrive; the gauche man with the lop-sided smile, the man whose shirt always pulls free from his waistband as he hurries his way from the station. Today, he's late. Madeleine tries to be patient. Tonight, Madeleine has prepared her surprise.

The platforms grow empty. The chilled night falls and still there's no sign of her love. She hears the rumble and screech of the night's last train as it barrels down the tunnels towards her. Madeleine's breath is stolen away. He is here. And Madeleine thrills to his touch as he steps down onto her platform, as his firm fingers grasp at her handrails. She is dizzy with love, with desire, as he strides through her tunnels and trots up her stairwells.

Madeleine bends her form through the earth, rearranges her corridors, diverting him down, spiralling deep into Madeleine's heart where she locks him safe in her concrete embrace. Outside, Madeleine

---

closes her gates to the world.

And, as one, all of her lights glow red with the passion of their love.

Barry Hale is a writer, arts producer and filmmaker. His past work includes music promos and moving image art, exhibiting extensively across Europe. For twenty years he was Co-Director of Threshold Studios, dedicated to assisting artists and filmmakers from underrepresented backgrounds to access opportunities in the arts and media industries. From 2011-21 he was Co-Director of Frequency Festival of Digital Culture in Lincoln. As a writer he navigates the dream-states, drawing on the dream journals he has kept for the past 40 years. He is currently writing a novel of contemporary magick based on genuine visionary experience.

The Devil's Song
by Molly Nash

If you follow the winding path as it lures you up the hill-

    through the gates of faces trapped beneath a waxy seal

    and past the tree stumps, charcoal grey, and screaming as you pass,

    be sure you make no peek behind or in the looking glass.

    'Cause if you do, the whites of eyes will mirror the whites of bone

    and the crunch of marrow and drip of blood will break the silent stone.

    But if you are the bravest sort, jerked on by strings of valour,

    and shrieks and moans and giggles of night stir nothing but your pallor,

    then creep along the winding paths, weave jagged teeth of graves,

    slide through the trees of charcoal grey and ignore their branches' waves;

    slip past the gate, and past those faces wrought in

iron core:

You'll meet the raven upon the hill who caws forevermore.

And in the darkness, the moon will hide, afraid of what she'll see,

another soul ripped from the chest and hung upon the tree?

The raven caws as black as death, an omen dark and strong,

and if you follow the winding path, you won't last very long-

because intrigue is the Devil's tool and you've listened to His song.

Molly is an avid writer of every genre and format, with the ambition to become a fully-fledged author as soon as possible! She has had a few short stories and poems published in a series of anthologies (her favourite of which was the Chris Salmon Poetry Extravaganza) and loves working out the tiny details in misdirection poetry more than anything else.

Last Lift

by Brian K. Bolen

Paxton gazed at the man as he approached; the man appeared homeless.

"Are you Sam?"

"Yeah."

You called for an Uber?"

"Yeah."

"Hop in."

"Thanks."

"Where to?"

"Take I-75 south and then take Exit 33."

Sam slid in behind Paxton, his eyes moving from side to side. Paxon shifted into drive and felt a muzzle pressed against his neck. He glanced into his rearview mirror and said, "Take it easy, Sam. There's no need for bloodshed."

"Fucking A, there isn't. Drive."

When they passed exit 27, Paxton heard a moan.

"What the fuck?" Sam said, removing a blanket. "You got a kid back here?"

"Yeah. He's my son."

"Like I care." Sam stared at the boy, eyes wide, frowning. "Why's he so pale?"

"He hasn't eaten."

"Not my problem." He looked at the boy, heart tugging. "Take the next exit and go through a drive-through."

"Yeah?"

"Yeah, I don't want him getting sick."

"Thanks." Paxton got into the right lane, but missed the exit.

"You passed it."

"I know." Paxton heard his son stirring. "Gavin—eat."

Fangs sprang out, entering Sam's neck. Sam shrieked as blood struck the windows in a maniacal spray. Sam slumped, dropping his gun. Pulling over, Paxon watched as his son fed.

Brian K. Bolen is a clinical psychologist, licensed marriage therapist, and addictions professional. He lives in Florida with his wife Erin and six glow light tetras. He has published five 101 word micro stories. During his spare time, he plays the saxophones and flutes, preferring Smooth Jazz and R&B.

Hunger Hurts
by Ari Boulting

Wasn't that love? That moment in the tent when our eyes met and we knew how things were going to be? Wasn't it adoration when you stood in front of me, shielding me from the cutting breeze, the gap in the canvas, and sliced into my arm? Wasn't it worship when you took me onto your tongue like the body of Christ and BIT?

Don't tell me it wasn't. Don't look at me like that. Don't turn away from me now. It's done. It was done, it is done. It was for love, so how could it be wrong?

I warmed you from the inside out, didn't I? Wasn't I a good wife? Didn't I keep you warm? Didn't I do what was best for us both? I know I did.

So don't fucking look away from me now, now that I'm cold. Now that I'm just enamel, ephemera.

Because I'm with you still.

Blood of my blood, my blood in your blood.

So I KNOW it was love.

Love of the wolf, love of the rope, LOVE, plain and simple. Thick, warm, red love in your throat. Love pouring out of me, because you never could clean up after yourself. That was love.

Wasn't it?

Marianne Graziela 'Ari' Boulting Williams is named after four dead people. They are studying for a BA in History in Brighton. When they have spare time, they write, draw, and listen to as many gay history podcasts as they possibly can. More of their work can be found @ariboulting on Instagram.

First Contact
by Scott McGregor

Captain Graham Kumar couldn't take his eyes off the lifeform, mesmerized by the vibrant rose-red gel. The CF-Olivera's fourteen-month space endeavour sought to sample Mars's surface, but little did the crew expect they'd return with extra-terrestrial life. Confined within the glass cage, it looked like liquid metal similar in property to mercury. After hours of examination, Dr. Telowski confirmed the gel was a living organism.

"The outer-core is unique, capable of rearranging layers to mimic substances," said Telowski

"Meaning?"

"Simply put, it's capable of copying the appearance of other organisms."

"Fascinating, I'll report to headquarters."

In the communication hub, Kumar heard a scream come from the laboratory. When he darted back, he found Telowski standing outside the door, blank-faced.

"What happened?" Kumar asked.

Telowski stayed silent.

"The hell's wrong with you, doctor?" Kumar ignored Telowski and entered the lab, afraid something jeopardized the lifeform. He found the empty, shattered cage, along with Telowski dead on the floor, throat slashed by glass.

The other Telowski strolled inside and met with Kumar. His skin turned a vibrant rosy red, becoming a liquid gel humanoid. Seconds later, the creature transfigured, and Kumar stood face-to-face with himself.

Holding the telecom, Kumar reported his final words, "Houston, we have a problem."

Scott McGregor is a Canadian author based in Calgary, whose fiction has appeared in Crystal Lake Publishing, Eerie River Publishing, Oddity Prodigy Productions, Hellbound Books, and many others. He recently graduated from Mount Royal University with degrees in English (Honours) & Sociology, with a minor in Creative Writing. His honours project explored Marxism in literature and the future of historical materialism. His upcoming novelette "Mr. Hangman" will be released in February of 2022.

Silent Motions
by Mara Lynn Johnstone

In retrospect, we should have spent more time translating the warning. The old languages had multiple meanings for common words, a fondness for flowery phrasing, and a compulsion towards cryptic jackassery on their cautionary signs. We thought this one said that only people who could be stealthy should enter — so we left our noisy gear outside, roped ourselves together, and walked single-file into the dark tunnels. My friend in the lead was the only one with eyes enchanted to see in complete blackness. I thought longingly of the night-vision goggles I'd had once. It was fine.

We were proud, stepping quietly so the monsters didn't hear. Breathing gently, moving so our clothes didn't rustle. We couldn't see a thing, but that didn't matter; we would reach the end soon. No one would know we'd been there.

Then my left wrist, stiff from all the careful walking, felt uncomfortable. I didn't think twice about rotating my hand to pop the joint ever so quietly.

It lit up like a glow-stick. My wrist was a bright green that illuminated every shocked face that my friends turned toward me.

Plan B was running. With more joints popping in exertion, and oh, they should have sent a child.

Mara Lynn Johnstone grew up in a house on a hill, of which the top floor was built first. She split her time between climbing trees, drawing fantastical things, reading books, and writing her own. Always interested in fiction, she went on to get a Master's Degree in creative writing, and to acquire a husband, son, and three cats. She has published two books and many short stories. She still writes, draws, reads, and enjoys climbing things. She can be found up trees, in bookstores, lost in thought, and at MaraLynnJohnstone.com

Our Fathers' House

by Stephanie Ondrusek

The chill shoots straight up from underground. It grows through the floor, runs its fingers through the shag carpet like hands through a lover's hair, curls its tendrils around my heart. I could never get warm inside this house, then or now.

Another night floating through hallways, tending the skeleton that kept us safe. I've lived countless lifetimes here, inside the manse our ancestors built. You did, too, though you carry on where I couldn't. I sigh when I see you in your robe in search of coffee. Do you think of me as the sun dawns through dusty windows? Remember how you always found the kettle on?

I hope so, even still.

I follow you downstairs like I did as a pigtailed little girl hanging on her father's every word. I ache for you to turn to look me in the eyes, just once. I always have. You close the kitchen door against the draft, and my hand reaches for the knob. Maybe today I'll follow you and finally catch your attention.

My fingers curl around brass, and I breathe, but I'm not supposed to. It hits me: it's you that's gone, and if I don't stop now I'll be searching forever, lost to time.

Steph Ondrusek has been disappearing into reading and writing for a lifetime. She reads, writes, and watches fantasy, horror, science fiction, and thrillers—best when combined. Steph is a student of human dynamics: having worked a decade as a health coach and recently transitioned to liberation work and consulting, her curiosity has led her to devote her life to the examination of power and people. She has published articles for women's health and lifestyle organizations, and her blog shows this transition in work and writing as it occurred.

Hypocotyl
by Thomas Farr

Thankfully, my face is still the same. The eyes, though. I lean towards the mirror. The sclera, once white and smooth as the albumen of an egg, is now a sickly, liverish hue that almost seems to swirl and churn with a kind of smoke or fog. And the pupils— *well, shit*. Sorry, ma . . . looks like I didn't get off scot-free after all. My pupils resemble nothing so much as a pair of darksome boreholes. Like apertures in a plastic mask, or empty volcanoes viewed from above.

'Oh, fuck.' I tug gently at an eye-corner. The skin stretches like taffy, deforming out of human shape. This isn't good.

I lean in closer. The small fluorescent striplight flickers in protest. As if it, too, would rather not see any more.

'*Fuck!*' I jerk backwards at the sight of it. Then, I lean towards the mirror again. In the inky cenote of one pupil, a vermiculate, cabbage-coloured tendril coils and uncoils quite languidly. Dozens, in fact—a veritable forest of milky strands, floating everywhere, gently undulating like specimens preserved in formaldehyde.

My eyeballs begin to prickle. Then to itch.

Tentatively, I touch one of the pupil-holes with a fingertip; and, tentatively, something touches me back.

Thomas Farr is a British writer of dark fiction and poetry. His work has appeared in The Dark Door, Eunoia Review, The Folkestone Anthology and elsewhere. Several of his stories have been adapted for audio, most recently for the Horror Hill podcast. When he isn't reading or writing you can probably find him in Silent Hill. Either that or he's getting a new tattoo. He tweets @TFarrHorror

A Room of Her Own

by Rosie Cullen

This house was old and large, Jess had a room of her own—no more sharing with Archie, hurray! But tomorrow there would be a new school. Her stomach tied itself in knots. They would all know each other and call her names like *shitbum* and *picklehead*.

Jess tossed with anxiety. In the middle of the night, a scratching came from beneath the bare polished floorboards. Her eyes opened wide. A mouse? She'd tell mum in the morning. The floorboards began to creak and strain. Jess sat up and pulled in her knees, she should tell mum now! By the glow lamp she saw one of the boards suddenly snap up. Jess gulped, could she jump over it from the bed? A small bony hand appeared. Too late. Long sharp nails groped at the edge of the flooring. The board broke away at last and a thin shadowy figure crawled out of the darkness. Not much bigger than a baby was Jess' first startled thought.

A pale face framed with lank strands of fair hair stared at her from dark sunken eyes.

'This is my room …' it whined.

Jess clutched her sheets, 'Couldn't we share?'

The creature frowned then smiled, showing its sharp little teeth.

Rosie Cullen was born in Dublin and now lives in Manchester, England. Her career has included theatre, front of house, and puppeteer but principally writing for theatre, film and TV. In recent years she has concentrated on prose, short stories and flash fiction have been published in various anthologies including, MONO, Glittery Literary, Worktown Words, The Copperfield Review etc. Her novel, The Lucky Country, was published in spring 2021.

Homework

by Ed Dearnley

Some people like their house toasty warm, but this was ridiculous. Every time I looked out of the window of our new house, I could see it: a white plume of smoke, rising from the chimney and drifting towards me on the breeze. A warm, sunny spring had arrived, but number fifteen just kept that fire burning.

Watching the neighbours was my new hobby. Number seven had a booze habit, adding six empty bottles to the neat stack on their driveway every morning. The dad at number nine was home-schooling, sneaking out at half-eleven for a cigarette and a silent rant. Number eleven were worriers, disinfecting their shopping bags on the doorstep before letting them anywhere near the husband's elderly mother. There was no number thirteen.

The thin-faced guy at number fifteen lived on his own. Word on the street was that he was a funeral director.

I was setting out on my daily walk when I finally spoke to him. He was in his front garden, planting bulbs. We nodded at each other and said hello.

"How are you holding up?" he asked.

"Ok," I said. "Just working from home."

"Me too," he said.

Our house went back on the market later that year.

Ed Dearnley lives in Sussex, where he works in research management and communication. He is the author of the non-fiction book London to Brighton Derailed.

Mother's Cookies

by L.M. Therrien

I'm trying to think less about how my mother's body is eroding in the damp Californian soil, harvester ants crawling between and through her toes, and focus more on her spirit. There was a flavor to her maternal love that is as real to me now as the scent of fresh baked cookies, which brings me to the kitchen. I stare down at a stain speckled ingredient card. My mother's famous oatmeal raisin recipe. The secret is to add extra cinnamon, it can cover even the strongest mistake. Of course, as an unconventional daughter I want to spice up this bare bones recipe by adding my own twist, so I grind raw things, wheat and oats, to give it that earthy taste.

I mix the eggs, leavening and penitence while swatting away gnats drawn to the bowl. I notice some larva clumping to a bit of dirt, but after tasting it realize it's just a buttery raisin.

Today I'll balance my inherited silver plate on her headstone and eat one cookie by her side, hoping her spirit will pass through me. And if I bite into a toenail shaped nutshell, I'll flick it back into the freshly churned grave and recall I didn't add any pistachios.

L.M. Therrien lives in the pacific northwest with her family. She explores the outdoors during the day and writes fiction in the evening. You can follow her on twitter @lm_therrien

Blood is Thicker Than Water

by Eve Keegan

Blood is thicker than water, I'm young enough to be your daughter, you hurt me once, you touched me twice, but thrice? It's time to slaughter. Blood is thicker than water, and dense enough it ought to, sink to the stones, where I'll leave your bones, I'll give no bloody quarter.

I bled you in a loch. I had to take time off work to cut you up. I let your meat simmer to the fat which I scraped into the garden incinerator bin, next to your scalp and middle-aged-man haircut.

I put your nasty bones in a bag, took a tour around your country in a car that doesn't go very well around corners and left a bit of you in each loch I stopped by. I hope their gentle tides ensure you never rest in peace; you'll rest in pieces.

I'm going to cry at your memorial and tell your mother through tears that I know you're still out there. You'll always be out there, and I hope it gets cold under that water. I know I made you suffer, I just wish I'd done much more. It wasn't enough.

All that and I can still feel your dirty hand groping at my breast.

Eve Keegan, 25, is an aspiring novelist, a keen poet, and mother to three rodents. She began her writing career at Falmouth University in Cornwall and since graduating has been working on a dark fantasy novel. Now living in Scotland, Eve enjoys yoga, soggy chips, and believes that a cup of tea can fix almost anything.

Grave Robbing
by Alex Kashko

Finished at last. Just three bones worth taking.

No point in nailing the coffin lid back down.

Here are the gates. What's that shuffling snuffling noise?

Close and lock the gates.

Put the finds into my cabinet of curiosities. Sleep.

Something taps at the window. Something falls with a thump to the floor. An enormous skeleton limps across the room. One finger missing from its right hand and it looks like some ribs are missing.

Can't move. It takes the bones I found from the cabinet. It turns to me, slings me over its shoulder we pass through the window.

Darkness and the smell of mould. Body disintegrating. Only bones left. Madness lures and seduces me.

A light and a figure sorting through my bones. It picks out three bones, sweeps the rest back into the coffin and goes. Stand up. Limping. A finger missing on my left hand. My feet complain of a missing bone,

He locked the gates. Wait till the moon gives me strength to pass through the gates. I feel the call from my missing bones. Pass through the window. Collect my missing bones

pick up the shivering figure on the bed and get back to my grave. I'll be free soon.

Alex Kashko used to write and design software, Now he writes poetry and occasionally fiction. His poetry has been published in Abyss and Apex.

Exit Strategy
by Ed Walker

Tony had had it, to overflowing, with people. With so much talking and unavoidable touching it was all he could do to keep himself from screaming or throwing up. Or killing. Killing himself or enough people to make space for himself on the ship.

Slipping out of his group sleeping quarters into a packed corridor, he tried to avoid contact with other people. In his fear and disgust he was carried along by the crowd until jumping into a doorway.

He found himself in an airlock, the one place people avoided. He closed the door. At last, a space with nobody else in sight, nobody's breath to dread inhaling. Just one other door between himself and oblivion.

Faced with two doors, he chose empty space. Tony quickly opened the outer door. His ears popped, the air rushed out and him with it. All he felt was relief. Alone at last.

With a start he recognized his body floating away. Relief was short lived as he could see other ghostly creatures all around him. A relentless stream of people, animals, plants, insects, fish, mushrooms, birds. Floating up to and - dear god! - floating through him. All eager to meet him, talk to him, share with him.

Ed Walker is a civil engineer and writer who lives and works in the Seattle area. He is looking forward to retirement and moving to Europe, where he can spend more time writing, relaxing with his wife, exploring the continent and entertaining their dogs. His work has appeared in The Arcanist and Grievous Angel.

Set in Stone
by Fern Lamb

I hate it when my knees crunch. They feel like jigsaw pieces that refuse to fit, and I swear they're chipping away, grinding into dust with each step. What even happens to it? Blending blood with powdered bone to produce some kind of cement? Setting joints at all the wrong angles?

Ugh.

I seem shorter, too. As if I've worn down an inch of marrow. My daughter says it's just my posture, but what can I say? Her dad, who built half the buildings in this town, can't lift the kettle? Can't hold his own granddaughter? This disease has already seeped into my foundations.

And it is crumbling.

Bones will break into shards. Shards will shred flesh. Flesh comes apart, and I'll come undone. Body snapping hard against cold kitchen tile.

I'll wail, no sound escaping from punctured lungs.

My phone out of reach. Daughter out of town.

That's it. That's how I'll die.

Limbs jutting outward before crumpling in. Back

arched in anguish. Shattered fingers gnarled and raking desperately for release, as if clawing through the foundations of my home will cure my own.

It's futile.

It'll crack.

It'll decay.

There I'll lay. Frozen in the throes of agony. Set in stone.

Waiting to crumble.

Fern Lamb is fresh blood, a keen writer looking to break ground. She has spent the past year collaborating with other creators in a community Comic Jam, writing scripts and putting out finished pages on a weekly basis. Recently, she has found new confidence in her written voice, opting to extend into narrative storytelling, with a focus on horror and dark fiction. https://thecomicjam.com/

Dead for Dessert
by Yii-Jen Deng

It happened in a little Parisian café, as sunlight caught the gleam of the spoon sinking into the strawberry blancmange. As she raised it to her lips, something blinked at her, bloodshot. She froze. The eye, watching wetly from the spoon, slid back and plopped into the glass bowl. Strawberry-pink eyelids drew over it and back, a tongue poked out, the eye spoke long and lugubriously: 'This is how it happened.' Aghast, she watched the blancmange absorb the eye with an awful squelching shudder, and what she hoped was dark strawberry sauce ooze out from where the silver spoon still stuck. Spectral wisps of steam began to rise. Through the glass, the fleshy-pink pudding could be seen churning and churning… with a start of horror, inside she could discern tiny bones and skulls that span erratically around, clanking manically, until they seemed to vanish like melting sugar. A door jangled open. 'Sorry I'm late!' said her friend brightly, throwing herself onto the curlicue chair. 'Blancmange, how lovely.' And she only stared, as a sliver of fleshy pink was scooped into the friend's mouth and how, before it closed, a bloodshot eye gazed balefully at her, as she licked her lips and asked the waitress for more.

Yii-Jen Deng is an English Language and Literature student who has previously written for Cherwell and The Isis. Her stories are often inspired by myths, food, and Virginia Woolf. She is based in Kent, loves trying to play the concertina, and has a funny corgi named Juno, who is afraid of cats.

It Hunts

by Noel Belmonte

It can see me. Even as it hides, its smell is overpoweringly close. I know what happens when it comes. I've seen my kin left grinning and in parts.

When it finally rises from the tall grass, I freeze. When a column of shadow falls on my back as it lurches towards me, I run.

It pursues. I turn as it lunges, again and again. I don't see the cliff face blocking my path until I'm backed against it. Caged.

I try to climb up but my arms are not made for this. I try to dig down but there's nowhere to go. It reaches and grabs me, squeezing. It holds me down and I fight, I push, I thrash with the desperation of the dying. Its hands are not made for this, no claws to dig into my flesh. I can slip away.

I'm faster than it, and I bolt to the open prairie, still nowhere to hide, but everywhere to run. It chases me, undeterred by my speed. My legs burn with strain but I can't stop. I can't let the exhaustion set in. When I slow down I can hear it, still behind, following. I can run faster, but it can walk farther.

Noel Belmonte is an Argentine speculative fiction writer based in Chicago. When she's not writing flash horror, she enjoys reading weird stories, taking on new baking projects, and staring down the dark expanse of Lake Michigan, its waters inscrutable, its icy winds bringing dread. You can find her on Twitter @NoelBWrites

Dark Switch

by A. N. Myers

There is an old man living in my attic. I say living—he doesn't eat, or drink, despite his ravenous expression. I shine my torch at him, and he dissolves like an image on glass.

The first time, I showed Sandra. He was crouching in the angle of the rafters, among the black bags, the heaps of insulation. She looked through him and said, 'You really need to lay that properly.'

If I approach him, he fades away. I can't get close. He shivers, thin and dusty, in his old man's jacket.

I wake. I can hear him moving around up there. I shake Sandra. 'Rats,' she says, and rolls over. I climb the ladder and he stares at me, lonely, accusing. The wind sighs around us.

I think I'm going mad. I can't tell anyone.

Sometimes I hear him humming, deep in the night.

Today he smiled at me. He seems to be edging closer, beneath the dim bulb, and he doesn't look so hungry now. A fat smirk fills his pale features.

The next time I go up I'll flick off the light switch. Join him. He can descend the ladder and take my place.

I won't be missed, up there in the dark.

A.N. Myers lives in London. His recently published fiction credits include 101Fiction.com, Speculative66, The Hammond House International Literary Prize, the Eibonvale Press Anthology "The Once and Future Moon", Sein Und Werden, and BFS Horizons. His His YA science fiction novel, "The Ides", is available from Amazon. He is a member of Clockhouse London Writers.

The Monster and the Rabbit

by Nik Lam

Alice's tiny, paint-covered fingers left messy prints along the floral teapot from which she poured tea for her vintage rabbit doll, Harvey. An old television blared her favorite movie. Her mother hurried down the basement stairs and stopped at the gruesome fingerpainting project left on the floor. A mess of crimson and brown. Four figures, one with bunny ears.

"Alice!" mother admonished.

"Harvey was thirsty!"

A door slammed from above. Heavy boots fell on the floor. Mother swallowed. The monstrous man shouted incoherent curses.

"Not a word. Just stay down here," mother hissed as she dashed upstairs. Alice hid under the staircase. The television barely masked the thumps and screams. The thud.

The monstrous man slurred, "turn that thing off!" as he reached the stairs.

"Make it stop, please," Alice whimpered, staring

at Harvey.

The basement lights flickered and failed. A shadowy figure moved from where Harvey sat, meeting the monstrous man at the bottom of the stairs.

"Who...wait a minute...I..."

A sickening crack ended the stammering. The monster dead, landing on the cement floor. The shadow reached for Alice's hand and walked her to the tea table. Bloody footprints tracked across the floor. Alice straightened her dress as she smiled.

"Thank you, Harvey. More tea?"

Nik Lam (she/they) is a sexuality, health, and wellness coach who writes horror and erotica and uses poetry as an emotional outlet when in the midst of an existential identity crisis. Born and raised in the Southern United States, she split her time between divorced parents, living in her mother's metaphysical shop while her father worked for a Christian church. She has written multiple horror short scripts for competitions and has several works in progress which focus on identity and trauma, obsession with perfection and self-imposed isolation.

Two Whispers

by Quinn Cary

I should never have come here, but I always knew that I would.

Strobing lights dazzle my eyes, the mass of dancing people an inviting slideshow of sweat and joy.

I should never have come here because I have a price on my head, and my bodyguards told me leaving the safehouse was death… but is eating oatmeal in a safe house for a year, surrounded by lifelessly silent men at every waking moment, truly living?

A beautiful woman dances alongside me, body tight and muscle toned. Her shirt rides up and exposes her belly, revealing a nine-millimeter in her waistband, glinting with her sweat. I dance with death, her every motion blending seamlessly with my own.

I don't know or care how death found me, I'm just glad it arrived in this form. They could have sent an assassin that would shoot me from a distant rooftop, caving in my unknowing skull–a merciful death, but not a personal one.

Death as I see her before me, shaking her waist with a devious smile, is as personal as she can be. The music stops and she whispers two things: one from her lips into my ear, and the other from her silenced pistol into my heart.

Quinn Cary is a Seattle-based horror writer, agnostic on the sun existing behind the rainclouds. He sleeps during the day and will be taken aback if you suggest he's a creature of the night, but he'll be flattered by your interest in his personal life, whispering "a gift of decent coffee for thee, and you will survive, you will be free.

Decision

by Geraldine R. Stoeckl

She swam about, thinking about what was coming. She had agreed to it, making plans, feeling optimistic. Now that it was closer, she had doubts creeping in, wondering if she had chosen wisely. Could she really do this?

The first part would go okay. After all, she would be helpless, and it would be what it would be, and as always, time would pass. The second part was more stressful because she could decide what to do. It was always scarier when you had a choice, no matter what they said.

She pictured the good parts. The love and hope she would feel being in his arms. She knew she had to follow at least part of this path, and the early times of their experience would be happy. But it wouldn't last, not once the alcohol became part of their lives. Then the abuse would begin, which would turn into violence.

Yes, she had agreed to it when everything seemed possible. When she thought she could be brave enough. It seemed to be a way to learn the next step in the whole process. Now, as she floated in the amniotic fluid, she knew that she had to decide whether to go through with it.

Geraldine R. Stoeckl is a writer, reader, and lover of all genres of fiction. She has traveled the world, and her non-fiction articles on travel and leisure were featured in the Air Force Base newspaper while living in Ramstein, Germany. Geraldine currently lives in Oregon with her cat, Ceta. This is her first short story.

A Gift Repaid
by Amanda Duncil

The blackbird is a missive. Wings akimbo, feet splayed. A calling card from a lifetime ago.

I ready the offering, stripping feather and flesh from bone. The stomach I fill with a soft exhale and anointed herbs, then set the makeshift balloon aflame on the altar.

The spell burns rancid, tendrils of smoke reaching to the otherworld to call forth my scribe. The room is suffocating, a charged electric current. I'm not alone. Maybe, I never was.

My hands trace protective wards automatically. "Show yourself, spirit. What are your demands?"

A laugh like char burnishes the floorboards. "I'm here to settle our debt."

I blink and the light goes with it, blotted out by void. Slowly, rippling edges stitch together comprehensible shapes: a series of limbs, an overlong torso, a head. Eyes like angry pustules erupt across its surface and train their fiery gaze in my direction.

The fiend has weakened since our last encounter, its form unstable and rapidly untethering from the mortal realm despite my efforts. A disastrous omen.

I speak its name as is customary. I already know what it wants.

"A soul for a soul," it demands. A callback to before.

I nod knowing I have no choice.

And then, I'm gone.

*Amanda is a writer based in Louisiana whose fiction has appeared in The Rumpus, The Toast, and recently in the R.L. Stine tribute anthology, It Came from Beneath the Ink! by ELJ Editions. You can find her online at www.amandaduncil.com **or** @amandaduncil.*

A Temporary Guest

by Alyson Tait

Every Halloween, I find a few teenagers with a Ouija board and take control of the planchette.

One of them always yells, but my eyes are on another. She simply stares — mouth agape.

My long-dead body sweats with the excretion of pushing the planchette around, but I get the girls to accidentally say a spell, one disconnected word at a time.

The quiet one squeaks out the final word of the seance. "Yes."

As soon as she finishes, something tugs behind my belly button. I'm yanked from my shadowy corner in foggy purgatory. In the blink of an eye, I'm staring at the ouija board from the wrong angle.

It's slightly blurry, and the light bounces back too brightly, but when I close my eyes, a hand violently shakes my shoulder.

Oh, I think as the screamer starts again. *They've noticed me already.*

"It's okay," I try to tell them. "I'm only here for one night."

I know that once Halloween ends, the universe will eject me back to where I belong. If they knew, maybe we could get along.

It's too bad I can't remember how to move a jaw. Instead of communicating, I cough up blood.

Oh well. It's not my body, anyway.

Alyson lives in Maryland where she got married, had her daughter, and began her writing journey. She has appeared in (mac)ro(mic), Wrongdoing magazine,HAD, and From the Farther Trees. You can find her on Amazon, and Twitter @rudexvirus1, and more works by her at her

Skeleton Dance
by Mike Deady

"The foot bone's connected to the leg bone."

God damn it, not again, Paul thought.

"The leg bone's connected to the knee bone."

He had been listening to the class sing that annoying song all morning while he chopped wood for the one-room schoolhouse's wood-burning stove.

"The knee bone's connected to the thigh bone."

He couldn't take much more of it. He knew they were singing it over and over again just to irritate him.

"The thigh bone's connected to the hip bone."

The little bastards thought they were so funny. They had even nicknamed him Paul Bunyan because he was the local wood cutter. Hilarious.

"The hip bone's connected to the back bone."

But they were just kids. The real problem was their teacher, Mister Pyper. He had had it in for Paul from the moment he arrived in town to take over as teacher. And now he was teaching the children to follow suit. Paul didn't like that at all.

"The back bone's connected to the neck bone."

Paul entered the classroom through the side door behind Pyper just as the children were singing the final line.

"The neck bone's connected to the head bone."

"Not anymore," Paul said as he swung his axe.

Mike Deady is a lifelong resident of Massachusetts. After a forty-two year career in engineering, he started writing fiction at the urging of his brother, Bram Stoker Award-winning author Tom Deady. Mike's work has appeared in Totally Tubular Terrors and Supernatural Drabbles of Dread. He is a member of the New England Horror Writers.

Jackie's Homemade Height Chart
by Safia Mlani

—(5ft. 8 in)

> *[Neatly printed in Nevada Department of Corrections standard Public Sans font, single spaced]*
> Inmate was executed at 0600 this morning for the brutal homicide and cannibalism of two hikers at Death Valley National Park.

—(5ft. 7 in)

> *[Blocky digits scratched into peeling wallpaper, few feet above streaky crayon bear]*
> Jack. Too old. Bad thing grew too.

—(5ft. 1 in)

> *[Typed amongst other physical descriptors on coffee-stained police report]*
> Juvenile runaway found on side of I-5. Claims to have sleepwalked.

—(3ft. 10 in)

[Scrawled on form labeled 'CONFIDENTIAL SCHOOL REPORT OF SUSPECTED CHILD ABUSE OR MALTREATMENT']
Bite marks on child's arms and legs; fresh. Guardian insists all were self-inflicted.

—**(3ft. 7 in)**

[Shaky digits in blue pen on halfway house wall]
MY feefth birthday God Bless AND keep away BAD THING

—**(3ft. 5 in)**

[Logged on hospital discharge form, above "SUMMARY OF PATIENT SERVICES"]
Emergency Forest Airlift Services, $22,450. Intensive Care Room, $5,600. Note: Outpatient pediatric psychiatric treatment recommended.

—**(3ft. 3 in)**

[Scribbled on doorway in faded sharpie]
Three year old Jackie before first camping trip!

—**(2ft. 10 in)**

[Neatly written in sharpie on the corner of freshly wallpapered doorway, below crayon bear]
Jackie's second birthday!! God bless Mommy's growing boy!

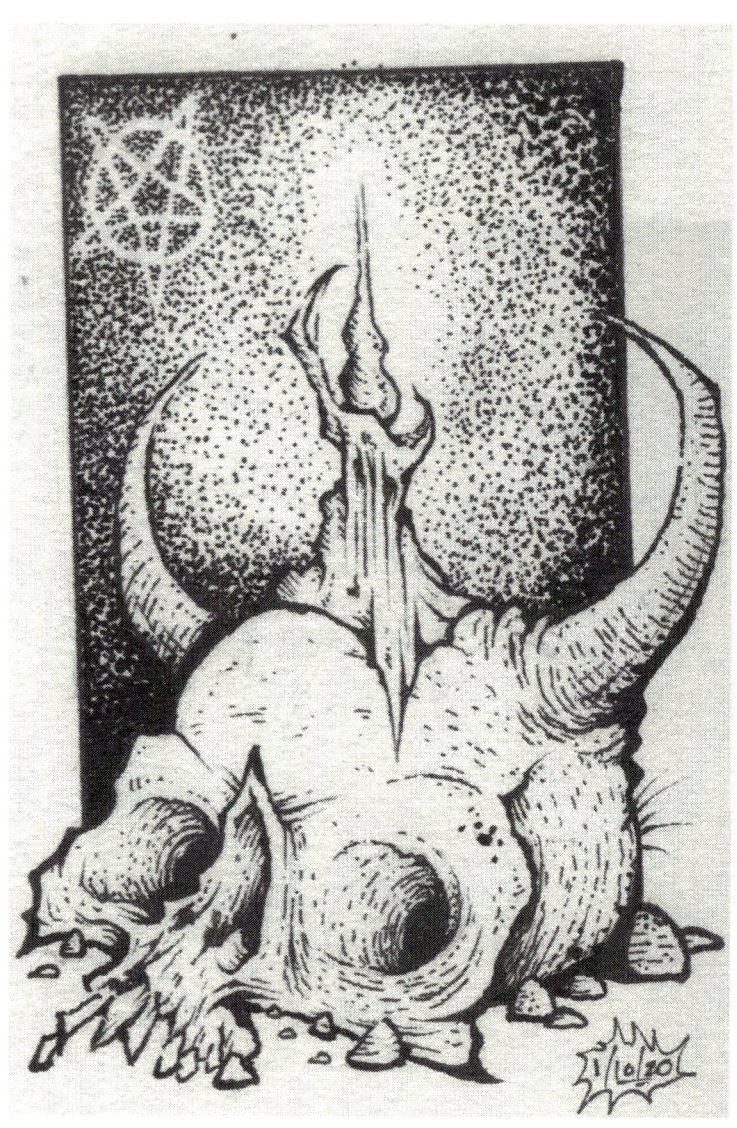

COMING SOON
FROM BAG OF BONES PRESS:

Annus Horribilis

An anthology of horror set in the shit show that is 2022.

Release date: May 2022

Thank you for reading this book.
Make no bones about it, we'll be back.

www.bagofbonespress.com
bagofbonespress@gmail.com
Twitter: @BagBonesPress
Instagram: @BagofBonesPress

Made in the USA
Middletown, DE
01 March 2022

61976095R00253